Deserted

"Do you by any chance know a family named Powell? It's a mom and her daughter, staying at the Ranger Rose. I'm leading them this afternoon on a hike through Canyonlands."

I shot a look at Sasha. Her face revealed nothing except my reflection in her sunglasses, but I knew that something was going on with her and the Ranger Rose. . . .

"Canyonlands," George murmured. "I hear it's fantastic—even better than Arches."

"It's bigger, but not necessarily better," Sasha countered. "Canyonlands is huge, stretching from north of Moab to way down south. You can drive to the rim of the canyon without a guide, but you need an expert to accompany you inside. Those canyons are like mazes, and many areas are remote and inaccessible, even to guides. It's an honest-to-goodness desert wilderness—extremely dangerous for novices." She wagged a finger at us playfully. "So don't go in there on your own, guys. Okay?"

NANCY DREW

girl detective™

Available from Aladdin Paperbacks

NANCY DREW

DREW
girl detective™

#7

The Stolen Relic

CAROLYN KEENE

Aladdin Paperbacks
New York   London   Toronto   Sydney

First Aladdin Paperbacks edition September 2004

Copyright © 2004 by Simon & Schuster, Inc.

ALADDIN PAPERBACKS
An imprint of Simon & Schuster Children's Publishing Division
1230 Avenue of the Americas, New York, NY 10020

Printed in the United States of America
20 19 18 17 16 15 14 13 12 11

NANCY DREW and colophon are registered trademarks of
Simon & Schuster, Inc.

NANCY DREW: GIRL DETECTIVE is a trademark of
Simon & Schuster, Inc.

Library of Congress Control Number 2003117087

ISBN 0-689-86843-X

Contents

The Stolen Relic

Mysterious Strangers

I was sitting around the house, reading this junky Western novel and recovering from my latest case, when my friend George Fayne dropped by with some interesting news.

Maybe a little too interesting.

"What! You've already made our plane reservations?" I cried, shooting up from the living room sofa. "What have you gotten us into, Fayne?"

"A fun time," George replied, with a toss of her short dark hair. "I saw this great airfare deal written up in today's paper. It includes a week in Moab, Utah, at a hostel called the Ranger Rose." She pushed a newspaper into my hand. "Here, Nancy. Take a look."

I glanced skeptically at the picture on the front.

Gorgeous red cliffs and strange rock formations popped out at me. A lone pair of hikers strolled down a wilderness path under a huge, deep blue sky. Above the scene a headline read, MOAB, UTAH: HIKER HEAVEN.

"Maybe you'll even find a mystery there," George added slyly.

I smiled. George knows how to grab my attention. I've never met a mystery I didn't like. In fact, I'm known throughout my hometown of River Heights for getting to the bottom of cases that stump our local police force. But I'm the first to admit the truth—there's no way I could solve them without a secret ingredient: friends. Three of them, specifically. George and her cousin Bess Marvin are my two best friends and co-sleuths, and my boyfriend, Ned Nickerson, helps me sometimes during his college breaks.

"Moab sounds awesome," George continued. "There are two national parks nearby, Arches and Canyonlands, with amazing hiking and mountain biking trails. There's also rafting on the Colorado River, horseback riding—every kind of wilderness sport you can think of. You've got to come, Nan. We have till tomorrow to phone in our credit card numbers."

Pushing back my shoulder-length strawberry blond hair, I cast my mind back to the sixth grade, when I wrote a report on national parks. Since then, I've been lucky enough to visit a bunch of them—Yellowstone, Acadia, Grand Canyon, you name it. But Arches and Canyonlands were unknown to me. I got curious.

"Maybe," I said, against my better judgment. I mean, hadn't I told Dad I'd help him do research this week? As a busy River Heights lawyer, he gets kind of stressed. Dad and I are close—especially because my mother died when I was three. So I like to make sure he's not overworked.

"Don't let me down, Nancy," George urged.

Outdoor adventures are George's passion. I wasn't surprised this vacation appealed to her. But did it appeal to me?

Her brown eyes scanned my face. I gave her back the article—and the thumbs-up sign.

"Yes!" George said. "And by the way, Nancy, that Western you're reading is perfect pre-vacation reading."

The rain pounded on the car like Niagara Falls on our way from the airport to Moab. I struggled to see the road ahead of me. A two-foot wall of mucky red water rolled toward us. A flash flood?

"Easy, Nancy," Ned urged as I fought to keep the car steady. "Keep your eyes on the taillights of that car ahead of us. Don't go too fast or we'll hydroplane off the road."

The wall of water hit us with a hard slap. I felt the car lift up, like a speedboat rolling through waves. If my throat had allowed me to choke out words, I would have croaked, "No traction!" Could a car make it through so much water? I clutched the steering wheel, hoping the current wouldn't sweep us away.

It seemed to defy the laws of physics, but the car kept plowing forward. Red water swirling. Rain pounding. Visibility, zero.

"If those taillights ahead of us disappear, it means a flash flood swept the car away," Bess said miserably.

"Stop it, Bess. You're making Nancy nervous," George said. Actually, not a word my friends could say would have made me nervous. The towering walls of water cascading down the cliffs surrounding us did that job just fine.

I held my breath, squinting, always keeping the taillights of the car ahead of us in sight. Our windshield wipers made a rhythmic *whoosh* sound as they swept the water back and forth.

"The rapids on the Colorado River will be awesome tomorrow," George declared. "Maybe we should go rafting instead of hiking."

"How can you think of sports at a time like this, George?" Bess moaned. "Our lives are in danger!

Haven't you heard about flash floods in the desert? They sweep away everything in their path—cattle, trees, cars."

"As long as the storm spares your suitcase, Bess, you'll be okay," George teased.

Bess shot her cousin a withering look, then studied the map, her long blond hair partly hiding her profile. It seemed like a million years passed, but finally I saw the neon sign of a Mexican take-out place shining through the rain, heralding the outskirts of Moab. No sight had ever seemed so welcome.

"Looks like we're finally in Moab, guys!" Bess crowed. "Three cheers for civilization."

Sometimes I can't believe how different George and Bess are, since they're cousins. Bess's idea of hiking is running to the next designer clothing sale, while George is a serious athlete. Bess is trusting, but George is skeptical. Bess is short while George is tall. The list of opposites goes on, but the great thing is that despite their differences, my friends are devoted to each other.

You may be wondering how George and I roped Bess and Ned into coming with us. I'm not sure what George said to Bess, actually. Maybe something about all the cute guys in Moab—bikers, kayakers, and park rangers. But whatever George did, it worked—Bess seemed eager to come. As for Ned, well, when he bought hiking boots at the River Heights mall the same day I told him of our plans, it seemed pretty clear to me that he wanted to come too. I would have invited Ned on the spot except I thought he still had exams. I'd forgotten the exact date they ended—three days ago. Anyway, I'm really glad he's with us. Flash floods don't seem quite as scary with Ned around.

The car ahead of us turned right at a crossroads, but that was okay with me. Civilization was popping up everywhere around us in the form of gas stations, fast-food restaurants, and ugly motels.

"The Ranger Rose is on Main Street," Bess said, consulting her map. "Just a couple more blocks." The fast-food joints soon gave way to unique little restaurants and stores, including a bunch of bike rental places. "There it is!" Bess cried, pointing to a beige adobe-style building with a painted rose over the front door. A red sign attached to the wall announced THE RANGER ROSE in script. A small parking area was on the left.

Ten minutes later we stood inside the lobby with our bags, totally drenched. The hostel wasn't frilly, but luckily it was clean and comfortable. Three guests shared each room, and there were bathrooms down the hall.

Outdoorsy types in rain ponchos wandered in and

out of the front door, unfazed by the weather, their faces tanned from sunnier days. This place had George's name written all over it. I wasn't so sure about Bess.

"Does it usually rain like this in Moab?" Bess asked the desk clerk, a deeply tanned young woman wearing a T-shirt with the words *Biking Fool* on it.

"Rarely," the clerk replied. "But don't worry, the sun will be out soon. The only clue that it's rained at all will be the crazy Colorado River. It's going to roll!"

George brightened. "How can we make reservations to go rafting?" she asked.

Bess groaned. "George, we've only just recovered from one life-threatening situation. Can't we just relax for a while?"

The clerk broke in. "I recommend hiking in Arches before you do anything. It's a great introduction to the high desert."

"The high desert?" Ned echoed. He brushed a lock of brown hair back over his eyes—a typical Ned gesture I've always been fond of.

"The Utah desert has a fairly high elevation," she explained. "It doesn't get quite as hot as the lower deserts like Death Valley in California. Also, there are mountains nearby with pine forests. You can go horseback riding on trails."

"Awesome," I said, eager to do it all. "But first let's

get settled, guys. After our long trip, I'm heading straight for a hot shower."

An hour later Bess and I waited for the others in the lounge downstairs, which was full of mismatched canvas chairs and Mexican rugs. I wore jeans and a black tank top with a green-and-pink beaded necklace. Hoping to influence the weather, Bess wore a turquoise sundress. A tall handsome dark-haired guy strolled in and shot Bess an appreciative glance. He was maybe nineteen. I reconsidered my earlier impressions of the Ranger Rose. Maybe this place had Bess's name on it after all.

He grabbed the chair next to us. "I'm Nick. Nick Fernandez. Did you girls just get here?"

Bess did most of the talking, introducing us and explaining how she was looking forward to all the wilderness sports this area offered. Nick lit up. "Maybe I can join you at some point, Bess. Especially if you go mountain biking. That's what I love most."

Ned and George hurried in, their hair still wet from showers. "Have you looked outside, Nancy?" Ned asked. "The sky's clearing."

Smiling, Bess and I introduced Nick to George and Ned, and the five of us chatted about a mountain biking race Nick had recently completed. "I came in third," he told us. "Got to do better next time."

"Don't be so hard on yourself, Nick," Bess said. "Third is great."

Before Nick could respond, a perky young woman with shoulder-length dark hair walked in, followed by a middle-aged woman with long gray hair. Nick introduced us to Priscilla and Margaret Powell.

Priscilla scratched her ski jump nose with its dusting of freckles. "Mom and I arrived at the Ranger Rose two days ago," she explained. "It's a small place—cramped, some would say—so all the guests are bound to meet. And by the way, please call me Missy." With her hair tucked neatly under a tortoiseshell band and her pressed khakis, Missy looked like the ultimate preppie. Margaret was different. Sporting patched jeans and multipierced ears, she peppered her speech with sixties expressions.

"We just arrived a couple hours ago," I told her as we shook hands.

"Groovy!" Margaret said, smiling. "Well, Missy and I are pleased to meet you. I hope you find Moab as far out as we do."

"Speak for yourself, Mom," Missy retorted.

Margaret ignored her daughter's rudeness. "Years ago, I hung out in a commune in the mountains nearby. We all lived in harmony with nature." Taking me aside, she added, "Missy's father and I are divorced.

She lives with him and his new wife in Southampton, New York, in a mansion the size of Buckingham Palace. Before this trip, Missy and I hadn't seen each other for several years. I'm not sure she approves of my lifestyle."

"Why not?" I asked, curious. Margaret sure seemed like an oddball. Why was she telling me, a perfect stranger, all this private stuff?

"I live a simple life on a farm in Vermont," Margaret went on. "I grow my own vegetables and raise goats to make organic cheese. I also run the local health food store. It's just not Missy's scene. The instant she went to college, she split."

"At least she agreed to come with you here," I said.

"I insisted," Margaret said, her chin set. "I left her some money in trust for when she turns twenty-one, but I wasn't going to let her have it if our relationship continued to be such a bummer. I do have a few rules."

Missy sidled up to us. "Mom, are you being honest? Are you telling Nancy that you dragged me here against my will?"

I stared at her. Why was Missy being so rude to her mother?

Margaret looked hurt. "Yes, baby, I brought you here. But it was to fix our relationship. You see, the desert has healing vibes."

"Mom, I need a dictionary to understand you," Missy said petulantly. "Are you ready for dinner? There's a sweet French restaurant I noticed down Main Street."

"Is it organic?" Margaret asked as she and Missy went out the door.

I stared after them. I'm used to plenty of eccentric characters in River Heights, but these two seemed wackier than most. I wondered if they always argued so much.

Nick turned to us. "Do you guys want to grab a burger?" he asked, glancing shyly at Bess. "There's a good place next door. Awesome chocolate malts."

"Perfect!" Bess pronounced happily. "I was worried at first, but Moab is working out just fine." And with those words, I relaxed. More than anything, I like knowing that my friends are happy.

We all returned from dinner around the same time. "Shouldn't French food take longer to eat than burgers?" George asked the Powells as we all fixed ourselves tea in the lounge.

"Not if you dine on salads," Margaret said. "I'm a vegetarian, and Missy wasn't in the mood to eat."

The detective in me perked up. "Really? Why not?" I wondered.

Margaret shrugged. "Ask her."

I was just about to obey when Missy plunked down her tea mug and glared ferociously at her mother, her lower lip trembling.

Uh-oh. Missy was spoiling for another fight.

"You act like you're so full of peace and love, Mom, but you're really just a control freak," Missy yelled. "Controlling me with your stupid money. Well, I don't need it. Dad gives me plenty!"

"Please, Missy, not now," Margaret said. "Not in front of others."

Missy clenched her fists. "Hypocrite!" she cried. "You're always telling me to let out my feelings— well, here they are! You never allow me anything I want. I'm leaving this dump. I'm going home to Dad and Mollie tonight!"

2

Heat Stroke

Missy stormed out of the room and pounded up the stairs. I glanced back at Margaret. She caught my eye and shrugged.

"What can I say?" she said. "My daughter is really uptight. Typical Aries, type A personality." She studied the tea bags in a basket by the hot plate. "Aha!" she cried, brightening. "I recognize this tea. It's a special herbal blend. Zaps bad moods, even hopelessly cranky ones."

As Margaret got to work brewing tea, Missy clumped down the stairs hoisting a suitcase. "Good-bye," she said stiffly from the doorway of the lounge. "I'm leaving now. The desk clerk is calling me a cab."

"Here you go, baby," Margaret said, handing her a steaming mug of tea. "My good-bye gift."

Missy rolled her eyes. "Woohoo," she muttered. I braced myself for a steaming hot mother/daughter confrontation. I could practically see Missy knocking the tea onto the floor. But much to my surprise, Missy dropped her suitcase and took the mug. After sniffing it suspiciously, she began to sip. Ned and I exchanged looks. I could tell he agreed that *strange* wasn't too strong a word to apply to Missy.

Five minutes later we were all drinking Margaret's tea in the lounge. But despite her prediction, everyone's mood remained low, especially Missy's. When the desk clerk announced the cab, Missy said, "Thanks, but I won't be needing it after all. Mom won her war. I'm staying."

I'd already been keeping my eyes peeled for a mystery in Moab. But the only one I'd found so far was this: How would the Powells spend another week together without driving themselves batty?

Bright sunlight shot through the windows in the room I shared with George and Bess. "Whoa, George, that's intense," Bess groaned, blinking. "Do you have to fling open the curtains?"

"It's nine in the morning," George said, already dressed in shorts and hiking boots. "If I hadn't opened these curtains, you guys would sleep till noon."

"What's wrong with that?" Bess asked groggily.

"Ned's awake too," George went on. "I ran into him downstairs at breakfast. We're both anxious to get out on the trails. Luckily, Arches is only a ten-minute drive away."

"Then let's go," I said. I was always eager to see Ned. I went straight to my suitcase and dug out my khaki hiking shorts, white tank top, and baseball cap. Then I shoved two water bottles, my trusty sunscreen, sunglasses, and a map of the area into my backpack.

After Bess and I finished our strawberry waffles downstairs, we joined Ned and George in the car. Each of us brought water bottles or canteens, having been warned by the desk clerk about the strong desert sun.

It was Ned's turn to drive, and as we started down Main Street, I craned my head around to get a sense of Moab in daylight. Small bookstores, cute restaurants, bike shops, and outdoor-equipment stores lined the sidewalks. Teenagers and college kids roamed around, wearing up-to-date hiking clothes. Some wheeled bikes. The scene reminded me of a beach town, except with bikers instead of surfers. Come to think of it, Margaret Powell was the only person over thirty I'd noticed so far in Moab.

"You're as good as your word, George," Bess said

from the backseat, scanning the pedestrians. "These Moab boys are *something*."

"You've already snagged one of them," George said, grinning.

"I was hoping to see Nick at breakfast. But no such luck," Bess said. George and I traded knowing glances. Our beautiful friend was in typical form—a magnet for handsome guys.

Soon Ned turned right into Arches. After paying our entrance fee, we continued along the road, scouting for the trail to Delicate Arch, which our guidebook told us was a must-see.

The road took us to the side of a cliff, then snaked through an endless plateau of amazing rock formations. I knew Utah would be beautiful, but nothing prepared me for the stunning landscape that stretched for miles on every side, right up to snow-capped peaks. The color of the earth was red, but it came in a zillion different shades. Bright red cliffs, rust-colored arches, and magenta spires were scattered like weird aliens everywhere we looked. And the sky above us was huge, like this blue upside-down ocean.

"This view is fantastic," I said, barely able to find words.

Ned pulled into a small parking area near the entrance to a trail. "Here we are—the trail to Delicate Arch," he announced. "The guidebook says it's sort of challenging, but not impossible. Perfect for our first day out. So does everyone have enough water and sunscreen? That's real important in the desert."

"I'm prepared," Bess said confidently, patting her canteen. She looked around, her blue eyes round with awe. "How were all these rocks formed?"

"Erosion," came a voice on our right. I turned toward it. A pretty young woman in a brown park ranger outfit smiled at us. A camera hung around her neck. Her long dark hair was pulled back in a braid, and I could see our reflections in her sunglasses.

"You mean the wind and rain carved all these shapes out of larger rocks?" Ned asked, surprised.

"Yup. Millions of years of wind and rain," the woman answered. "The geological history of this area is fascinating. Many millions of years ago, this area was all under the sea. Some of this stone is ancient sediment."

"Incredible!" George exclaimed.

"The Southwest is known for being the home of a prehistoric tribe called the Anasazi, whose civilization flourished here from around one hundred to thirteen hundred A.D. But the Anasazi are brand new compared with these rocks." She held out her hand. "By the way, my name is Sasha Starflower. I'm a park ranger and guide here."

"Sasha Starflower—what a pretty name!" I said as we shook hands.

17

Sasha's giggle was infectious. "Thanks. Lots of people tell me that. My mom is British, and she always liked the name Sasha. My dad is Navajo Indian. Starflower is his surname."

After we introduced ourselves, Bess said, "Our names aren't as poetic as yours."

"Native American names can be very descriptive," Sasha said. "I have a friend who runs an antique shop in Moab named Andy Littlewolf. I always liked that name. He's Navajo too."

"Are there a lot of Navajo around Moab?" George asked.

"Our reservation is south of Moab. Mostly it's in Arizona, but some of it crosses the Utah border. That's where I grew up—in Monument Valley. My parents still live there. Actually, the Navajo reservation is the largest one in the country."

"If it's anything like this," I said, gesturing, "it must be gorgeous."

"The Southwest is unique," Sasha said. "There's no land quite like it anywhere else on Earth. I'm glad you guys could visit. Here, let me show you some petroglyphs. I've been photographing them."

"Petro*what*?" George said.

"Carvings and pictures left mostly by the Anasazi culture centuries ago," Sasha explained. She beckoned for us to follow her up the trail. "Along the way to Delicate Arch, there are some petroglyphs of sheep and horses. Of course, there weren't any horses in the New World until the Spanish brought them here. So these petroglyphs came after the Anasazi. But maybe they influenced the technique."

I took a sip of water, then filed behind Ned as Sasha led us forward. After a few minutes, we came to a small cliff where an illustration of horses, sheep, and humans appeared on the wall in what looked like a hunting scene.

"I'll have to show you some true Anasazi petroglyphs sometime," Sasha said. "It's hard to believe how old they are. They came before the Black Death in Europe, around the time of the Crusades."

"What happened to the Anasazi after thirteen hundred?" I asked.

"*That's* the million-dollar question," Sasha said. "No one really knows the answer. For years archeologists have searched for clues. One day the Anasazi just packed up and went. But they left a lot of their stuff behind, almost as if they expected to return the next day."

George nudged me. "A mystery for you, Nan," she whispered.

I have to admit I was intrigued. But how could anyone solve this mystery when the witnesses and suspects had been dead for seven hundred years?

"Maybe a conquering tribe drove them out, like the Navajo?" I suggested.

Sasha shook her head. "The Navajo came to this area long after the Anasazi disappeared. We're actually newcomers to the Southwest. We arrived around the same time Columbus was making his trips to America. We migrated from way up north."

She shielded her eyes from the sun as she spoke, causing her jewelry to sparkle in the sun. "What a pretty ring, Sasha," Bess said, pointing to a silver ring with a large turquoise oval on Sasha's hand.

"Thanks, Bess," Sasha said. She took off her sunglasses to examine it, then glanced back at us with her beautiful large dark eyes. "It's Navajo of course. Our tribe is known for making jewelry and other crafts, like rugs and baskets. My dad gave it to me when I turned twenty, several months ago."

The sun climbed higher, and I was beginning to feel like burnt toast.

"Thanks for all your great info, Sasha," I said. "We'd better get going before the heat bakes us. Maybe we'll see you around later."

Sasha smiled. "I hope so, Nancy. If you ever need a guide for the more remote trails around Moab, please let me know. I know this area like the back of my hand."

We headed up the trail as the sun poured down on

us. I took out my sunscreen and slathered it over my face and arms. We all rationed our water. What was that comment the desk clerk made about the high desert being cooler?

Soon we crossed a gigantic rock textured like the moon's surface, with small stone cairns as markers. Not a soul was in sight.

"This place is freaky," Bess said, scanning the horizon. "Where are the other hikers?"

"Fortunately not here," George said. "That's why it's so cool."

"Cool? I've never been hotter," Bess retorted. "And we could easily get lost. No one would ever find us."

"I bet Sasha would," I said. "Sounds like she's an expert tracker."

"Delicate Arch is around this corner," Ned said, striding onto a narrow ledge that straddled a giant cliff.

Moments later Delicate Arch rose before us on a stony plateau. We walked up to it. Hot and tired, we couldn't believe how amazing it was. It was as if we were in the presence of a magic vision. The arch was a rusty red and huge, but it was also graceful. Its base was narrower than its height, so it looked as if it might topple over in the next breeze. Though the air was still, I backed away. I'm a firm believer in hedging my bets.

"I can't get over that the wind and rain did this," Ned said.

I'd read in our guidebook that Delicate Arch was like a pilgrimage destination for some people, so I wasn't surprised to find Margaret Powell sitting cross-legged underneath it, a goofy faraway smile on her face. Missy slumped next to her, looking even more bored than she'd looked yesterday.

"Hey there, folks," Margaret said the moment she noticed us. "Have a seat."

"No thanks, Margaret," Bess said. "I'm really hot and there's not much shade. I've really got to start back."

"Us too," I said, elbowing Ned as he was about to sit. Bess is usually an excellent sport, willing to put up with more than her share of discomfort when something really matters. So I took her complaint seriously. "It's almost noon, and I'm running out of water," I added. "'Bye Missy, Margaret. See you guys back at the Ranger Rose."

"Let's go, guys," Bess said, starting along the path.

Ten minutes passed, and we found ourselves back on the rock face, scouting for the markers so we wouldn't lose our way. The sun beat down mercilessly. The air shimmered with heat. Even with my hat on, I felt roasted. Were we really still on Earth, or had we jumped to Mercury while I wasn't looking?

"My head is swimming," Bess announced.

I looked at her. Her fair-skinned face was beet red. Drops of sweat trickled down her temples. "Here, Bess, have some water." I fumbled to unscrew her canteen and held the spout to her lips.

She gulped it.

"Let's find some shade," Ned suggested.

"Where?" George asked, scanning the treeless plateau.

Bess wobbled forward, her face still flushed. "I don't think I can make it any farther."

"Let me carry you," Ned offered. But before he could scoot over to her, Bess crumpled into a heap on the baking ground.

3

Bad Behavior

Water!" George exclaimed, kneeling** by Bess. Bess's canteen had fallen with her, and the water was trickling onto the dirt. Ned dove to save it as I scanned the plateau for help. A few hikers were coming toward us, but they were the size of ants. Hopelessly far away.

"Help!" I shouted anyway. The heat was muddling my brain, but I forced myself to focus on our options. I willed my legs to take me across the rock face toward the hikers.

"Nancy, what's wrong?" came a voice on my right. "I was looking at nearby petroglyphs, but then I heard you!" I turned to see Sasha moving toward me from a group of large cylindrical rocks not too far away. Phew.

"Bess fainted," I explained as we met up "I'm worried she's dehydrated. But I don't know why she would be, since she just had water."

Sasha frowned. "Has she eaten anything recently, like nuts or a salted snack?"

"Nothing since breakfast."

"Then she must be dehydrated. I know exactly why," Sasha said with a decisive nod. "Let's go." We rushed back together. Once we reached Bess, Sasha took out a bottle of liquid from her backpack. Holding Bess upright, she opened her mouth and dribbled the liquid in.

Ned, George, and I crowded around, willing Bess to wake up. Just when I began to worry that she wouldn't, her eyelashes fluttered open. The bright turquoise blue of her eyes was the best sight I'd seen all day.

Bess glanced around with a drowsy, vacant look. Then, to our dismay, she shut her eyes again. "Bess, don't give up," I said, squeezing her hand. "Sasha's here to help. She knows what to do for dehydration."

Bess groaned, opening her eyes.

"Good girl, Bess," Sasha murmured, pouring a little more liquid down her throat. "I think you're ready for the main course now—a handful of salted nuts." She fished out some trail mix from her pack and fed it slowly to Bess. Then she poured some extra water into Bess's throat and splashed it over her face. Bess perked up, her eyes widening with surprise.

"Excellent!" Sasha declared. "Let's get you to some shade."

Moments later Bess was resting in the shade of a nearby cliff. It was now afternoon, so the cliffs were casting shadows again.

"What was in that liquid you gave her?" I asked Sasha. "It was like miracle water. Bess's own water didn't revive her like that."

Sasha smiled. "I mix a little salt, sugar, and certain minerals into my water bottle because water alone won't stop dehydration—you need salt to absorb the water."

Sasha was amazingly cool under pressure. And her survival skills were awesome. She talked to us a bit about dealing with hiking emergencies in the desert, like what to do when you get lost and go through all your supplies. She told us about all these non-poisonous plants, and ways to find insects for moisture and nourishment. She also gave us tips on how to find our way back. "The desert is pretty unforgiving," she added solemnly. "The temperatures are extreme, and there's very little shade. You have to know what you're doing, even when you're on a short hike like the one to Delicate Arch, just over a mile."

"A mile doesn't seem very far," Ned said.

"When you're walking through a cool pine forest with plenty of shade, a mile is a snap," Sasha said. "But in the hot desert, a mile can be quite challenging. My dad got lost once in Monument Valley. For a while he wondered if he'd have to dine on some juicy bugs."

"Yuck," Bess said.

I grinned at her. Her attitude told me she was feeling a whole lot better. In fact, it wasn't long before she staggered to her feet and we took turns supporting her on our way back to the car.

"Where are you staying in Moab?" Sasha asked us as she helped Ned carry Bess.

"The Ranger Rose," I said. "It's a youth hostel in town."

Sasha's eyes clouded over. She opened her mouth to speak, then seemed to think better of it. A less observant person might not even have noticed her trouble. But I'm not a detective for nothing. And this was the first time I'd ever seen Sasha lose her cool.

The moment passed. Sasha forced a smile. "What a coincidence," she said smoothly. "Do you by any chance know a family named Powell? It's a mom and her daughter, staying at the Ranger Rose. I'm leading them this afternoon on a hike through Canyonlands."

I shot a look at Sasha. Her face revealed nothing except my reflection in her sunglasses, but I knew that something was going on with her and the Ranger Rose.

"Canyonlands," George murmured. "I hear it's fantastic—even better than Arches."

"It's bigger, but not necessarily better," Sasha countered. "Arches is rich in unusual rock shapes and, well, arches. And it's got some terrific trails and views. Canyonlands is huge, stretching from north of Moab to way down south. You can drive to the rim of the canyon without a guide, but you need an expert to accompany you inside. Those canyons are like mazes, and many areas are remote and inaccessible, even to guides. It's an honest-to-goodness desert wilderness, extremely dangerous for novices." She wagged a finger at us playfully. "So don't go in there on your own, guys. Okay?"

Back at the car we all thanked Sasha for her help. Soon we were on our way back to Moab. Bess sighed. "It's way past noon, and I sure could use lunch," she declared. "What about starting off with an ice-cream sundae at that soda shop down the street, then working our way back to the sandwich course?"

I laughed. Bess has a weakness for sweets. Her curvy figure attests to that. Of course, we all wanted to indulge her, so we did exactly as she asked. No big sacrifice on our part!

That afternoon, for Bess's sake, we decided to hang around the pool at the Ranger Rose. Shaded by cottonwood trees in a quiet interior courtyard, the pool's water shimmered with the little light that slipped through the leaves. The hardest work we did all afternoon was to slather on more sunscreen. After our crazy drive from the airport yesterday and Bess's fainting spell, though, I was happy to spend a relaxing afternoon by the pool.

"This is the life!" Bess said, dangling her legs over the side of the pool while Ned and George swam laps. "I'm only surprised you haven't found a mystery yet, Nancy. We've been in Moab for almost twenty-four hours. Do you think we'll actually get to spend a vacation just chilling out?"

I grinned from my deck chair behind her. It wasn't as if I hadn't been looking for a mystery. But I didn't want to upset Bess by admitting such a thing. "You mean, a mystery hasn't found *me*, Bess," I told her. "I'm perfectly content to be hanging out here right now. No danger, no trouble."

"No *fun*," she answered slyly. "I know you, Nancy. If you don't find a mystery by tomorrow, you'll be as bored as a caged cat!"

"Try me," I said, tilting my face toward the sun.

. . . .

That evening the four of us ate dinner at the Laughing Tortilla, a Mexican restaurant a block away. "Hey, isn't that Nick?" Bess asked as we stood in line waiting for a table. She nodded toward the take-out counter nearby. A tall, slim, dark-haired guy was leaning on it with his back to us. He wore bicycle shorts and a T-shirt covered with red dirt. I guessed from his three-quarter profile that it was Nick. There couldn't possibly be another guy in one little town who was so handsome—except for Ned, of course.

"Nick!" Ned said amiably as we all approached him to say hi. "Let me brush off your shirt."

Nick whirled toward Ned. "Keep away from me!" he snapped, his face an angry mask. "I don't need your help. I fell off my bike today, that's all!"

4

Missing

I put a reassuring hand on Ned's shoulder when he backed off in surprise. Bess, George, and I were just as shocked. Nick's outburst was totally unexpected for such a normally friendly guy. A mother would have used the word "unacceptable" to describe a toddler who'd acted like that.

"Nick, what's the matter?" Bess asked, stepping over to him. Surprised as she was, her forgiving nature helped her switch gears. "Ned was just trying to help. I'm sure you're an awesome biker. No one thinks you're a klutz for falling. In fact, I was wondering if you could give me a mountain biking lesson one of these days."

Nick softened, gazing at Bess's smiling face. He

seemed almost sheepish about his tantrum. But then I opened my big mouth.

"Wherever you go, just make sure there's shade." I described Bess's fainting spell, then added, "Fortunately, we met this really smart, nice ranger named Sasha who came to her rescue."

You would have thought I'd mentioned his most embarrassing secret or something. Nick's handsome face contorted into a hideous scowl. He turned bright red, stared at us with furious steely eyes, then stalked out of the restaurant just as the cashier called out his name.

"I wouldn't bother to keep his order warm," Ned mentioned to her. "Something tells me he's not coming back."

"Weird!" George said. "Why would Nick fly off the handle like that?"

I didn't have an answer. Thanks to Nick, the four of us were silent while we munched on nacho appetizers at our table. But nothing can keep the four of us quiet for long. By the time our main course arrived, we'd already cheered up. We took turns guessing what was bothering him.

"It's nothing," Bess said with a wave. "Maybe his shoes were too tight."

George snorted. "Maybe you're too forgiving! No, Bess, something is definitely up with that guy."

"It's as if he has two personalities," Ned said, putting down his soda. "Good and bad." He turned to me and smiled that warm Ned smile I love so much. "What do you think, Nancy? You're the detective."

I sighed. I always hate to disappoint Bess, but I try to be honest with my friends. It's a matter of honor.

"I agree with Ned and George," I said. "Nick's behavior was too strange to shrug off. I've been a detective long enough to realize there's always a reason for someone's weird behavior."

"Maybe his back hurt him. He'd fallen, hadn't he?" Bess said as our desserts arrived. "I mean, the reason for his mood doesn't have to be mysterious."

"Maybe. Maybe not," I said. But my curiosity was on high alert. Something told me Nick's anger wasn't caused by a bad back or tight shoes. I was willing to bet it was caused by something a whole lot deeper.

After dinner we strolled back the Ranger Rose. The evening was crisp, which George mentioned was typical early summer weather in the desert—hot days and chilly nights, thanks to the low humidity. A full moon lit our way, and the sky was thick with stars. The Milky Way was a swath of white, like a cup of overturned milk. I wondered what the Anasazi Indians had thought of this sky when they lived here a thousand years ago. Like all people, they probably had their own special stories describing how the night and the stars had been made.

A hall clock chimed ten as we opened the hostel door.

"I wonder how the Powells enjoyed Canyonlands," George said. "I'd like to hike there one of these days."

"Let's check out the lounge," Ned suggested. "If they're there, we can ask them." But George and Bess decided to go up to bed. Bess was especially tired after her eventful day.

After Ned and I bid them good night, the desk clerk, this time a young man, said, "Did I hear you guys mention the Powells? You know, they haven't come back from their hike yet, and I'm getting a bit anxious."

"Maybe they went straight from Canyonlands to dinner," I said.

"Unlikely," the clerk said. "See, Margaret asked me to hold on to her purse for safekeeping. She didn't want it weighing her down on her hike. But she'd need it for dinner. Plus, most people like to shower after hiking. You can get pretty grubby out there."

I felt a pinprick of worry. The desk clerk made sense. But Sasha was with the Powells, and Sasha would know her way back. Wouldn't she?

Before I had time for more guessing, the front door burst open. Much to my relief, Missy and Margaret stumbled in. But something was wrong. Blisters covered their faces and arms, and their lips were cracked and swollen. Despite their tricky relationship, they clung to each other for support, wincing from their terrible sunburns. It was painful to watch.

"Water!" Margaret croaked, collapsing onto a nearby bench.

Remembering Sasha's lesson about salt and sugar, I brought them some trail mix packets along with the water. They took everything from me with trembling hands, consuming it as quickly as their parched lips would allow. Missy was the first to recover well enough to talk.

"It's a miracle Mom and I are alive after Sasha ditched us!" she cried.

I gaped at her. A horrible thought went through my mind. "But . . . where's Sasha now?" I asked, dreading the answer.

"Who knows?" Missy said. "Like I said, she ditched us."

"You mean she just walked away from you?" Ned asked before trading a worried look with me.

"She went to investigate noise in some underbrush," Missy explained. "Or so she said."

Margaret took a breath. "Sasha was afraid the noise might be wild animals lurking around. Dangerous ones," she explained in a crackling voice. "So she went to check it out. When she didn't come back, we tried to find her, but with no luck."

"Well, did you call the police or the ranger station?" I asked.

"No!" Missy snapped. "I mean, what do you expect, Nancy? We just got home this minute. We barely found our way out of the canyon in the pitch black. We're dying of thirst and sunburn. And we were lucky. What if that noise *had* been a wild animal?"

I stared at Missy, horrified. What was this pair thinking? Even after they were safe, they cared more about their own problems than they did about Sasha. Canyonlands was no joke. Sasha had said it's a harsh desert wilderness. People could die there from thirst and exposure. And even experienced guides like Sasha could get lost—she'd compared it to a maze, not for novice hikers.

I pivoted toward the front desk. The clerk looked at me with frightened eyes. "I heard all that," he said. "Let's call the police, pronto."

He picked up the phone and punched in some numbers. After reporting Sasha missing, the clerk handed the phone to Margaret.

I hovered nearby. From what I could hear of the conversation, Margaret was describing where she'd last seen Sasha, but her manner was way too vague to be helpful.

Ned cupped his hand next to my ear. "Do you think the police will understand to look for her in Utah?" he whispered.

Margaret hung up. "The police are sending out a search party right away," she told us. "Missy, let's get to bed. We need rest. And I want to put some scallion ointment on our sunburns. If you ask me, this day has been a total bummer."

The desk clerk threw the Powells a disgusted look as they left. I was just as upset. "What can we do to help Sasha?" I asked him. "Right now, she's wandering in Canyonlands in the darkness, hungry and lost. Not to mention the poisonous snakes and coyotes. And it's cold! She must be terrified."

"The only people who can help Sasha are the rangers searching for her," the clerk said gravely. "They're professional trackers, and we're not. I think you should get some rest, then tomorrow you can go to the ranger station and ask what you can do."

The moment we all woke up the next morning, I told George and Bess about Sasha. Needless to say, they were horrified. "Maybe she's been found by now," Bess said, pulling on her jeans.

"Hope so," I said. "Let's go to the ranger station at Canyonlands and get some news."

While Ned was getting directions to the park from the front desk, Nick approached us from the lounge. "I was hoping to see you guys today," he said amiably. "I want to apologize for my inexcusable behavior last night." He flashed an embarrassed smile at Bess. "I hope you'll find it in your hearts to forgive me." He said "hearts" but he really meant one heart—Bess's.

"'Course we will, Nick," Bess said. "Don't even think twice about it. Look, we're on our way to Canyonlands to find out if this missing ranger has been found. If she's still lost, they may need search parties. Do you want to come too?"

Nick looked uncomfortable. "I heard about that ranger from the Powells this morning. Sasha Starflower, right?"

Bess nodded, and Nick went on, "I, er . . . know her, sort of. Sure, I'll come along with you. Hope she's okay."

I shot a look at Nick. Why the stutter when Bess mentioned Sasha? But I didn't have time to pursue the small mysteries when there was suddenly this big one on my hands.

The twenty minute drive to the ranger station on the northern canyon rim was quiet. Bess kept her flirting in check.

As I opened the door of the station, my stomach clenched. I held my breath, fervently hoping we'd hear good news.

5

Navajo Turquoise

The **ranger on duty** was an older man with gray, sad-looking eyes. I hoped that wasn't because of any bad news he'd heard. We all introduced ourselves and told him why we were there. I braced myself for the worst.

The ranger shook his head glumly, and my heart sank. "Sorry, kids," he said in a deep, gravelly voice, "we've found nothing so far, not even a shred of Sasha's clothing."

The door opened behind us, and a tall, middle-aged man with shoulder-length jet-black hair rushed in, followed by a pale, blue-eyed woman. She wore her light brown hair swept up in an elegant French twist. They were both dressed neatly but informally in khaki shorts, hiking boots, and polo shirts. The woman peered at the ranger, her face tilted expectantly, her eyes like lasers.

No words were spoken, but the instant the couple read the bad news in the ranger's face, they collapsed onto a nearby bench, too shaken up to speak.

I studied them. The man's dark eyes and high cheekbones resembled Sasha's, while the woman's graceful figure and quick gestures were just like Sasha's too. I realized they were her parents, and my heart went out to them.

The ranger spoke. "Mr. and Mrs. Starflower, I'm sorry, but we haven't found Sasha yet. We're doing everything we can to find her. Rest assured, we have several search parties working in the area where she was last seen."

"Oh, thank you so much," Mrs. Starflower said in her crisp British accent. "The instant we heard from the Utah police that Sasha was missing, we drove straight up here from Monument Valley. We were hoping you'd have good news for us by the time we arrived, but . . ." Her voice trailed off, and she blinked back tears.

I felt something brush against the backs of my knees. It was Nick, crouching behind me. He put his forefinger on his mouth as I shot him a questioning look.

No one else seemed to notice him. Meanwhile

Mr. Starflower put his arm around his wife. "I'd like to help search for Sasha," he told the ranger.

Nick made a creaking noise behind me. Everyone's attention spun toward him. But not before he was halfway out the door.

Like a cat pouncing on prey, Mr. Starflower lunged toward Nick, his face twisted with rage. What a difference from his friendly expression of moments before. "Nick Fernandez!" he cried, grabbing Nick's collar. "Have you been hiding here this whole time?"

"Hello, uh . . . Mr. Starflower," Nick sputtered. "I'm not exactly, um, hiding."

"Don't lie to me, young man!" Mr. Starflower said. "You want to avoid me. Why else would you be sneaking out the door like some snake?"

"No sir, I mean, yes sir," Nick said, his eyes darting toward me and my friends. "It's warm in here, and I was feeling claustrophobic."

Mr. Starflower glared at Nick, his eyes cold with scorn. "You're lying. You haven't changed a bit since you dated my daughter."

Nick twisted away. "You never liked me. You never gave me a chance!" he shouted. "I never lied to anybody. I miss Sasha. I love her!"

I looked at my friends. Nick loved her? This was news.

Mr. Starflower let go of Nick's shirt. His eyes

narrowed. "You don't know the meaning of love. If you really loved my daughter, you wouldn't have lied to her. And you've got some nerve coming here at this painful time. You're only making things worse."

Nick turned red with fury. His fists clenched at his sides. I could tell he was trying to control himself, but his anger was too explosive. With a white-knuckled fist, he aimed at Mr. Starflower's face.

Sasha's father flinched while Nick hit the air, his fist missing its target by an inch. We all held our breath, bracing for another punch—a real one.

Instead Nick slumped forward, his tension draining away. Then he stormed out the door, slamming it furiously behind him.

Mr. Starflower stared after him, as if he expected Nick to hurl the door open again. But after a few seconds of quiet, we all relaxed. That is, if it's possible to relax when a woman is missing in the desert and the temperature is climbing toward 95 degrees.

The ranger broke the silence. "That young man has some temper," he said. "He's got strong muscles, too. I'm glad he didn't hurt anyone."

"Me too," Bess said, shaking her head in disbelief. She cupped her hand by my ear and whispered, "Maybe Nick's outburst last night wasn't so out of character."

"Do you think he'll wander into Canyonlands

looking for Sasha by himself?" Ned wondered. "He's upset enough to do something rash."

"No," Mrs. Starflower said. "He'll probably hitch-hike back to Moab. Nick's a survivor, that's for sure."

We let that comment hang in the air. Maybe Nick was a survivor, but was Sasha?

I sat down on a worn sofa next to my friends, facing Sasha's parents on their bench. "Maybe I missed some-thing," I began, "but I had no idea Sasha and Nick went out with each other." I cast my mind back to yesterday when we'd told Sasha we were staying at the Ranger Rose. She'd seemed troubled. Was that because she knew Nick was staying there too?

"We met Nick at the Ranger Rose two days ago," Bess explained to the Starflowers. "Not once did he mention he knew Sasha—not even when we told him we'd met her." The flat tone of her voice told me she was trying hard not to sound hurt.

"Or when we told him she was lost," George said.

"I've never trusted Nick," Mrs. Starflower de-clared. "From time to time Sasha would complain he'd lied to her outright, but mainly he just hid the truth. That can be just as dishonest."

"They're not still dating, are they?" Bess asked.

"Oh, no, they broke up about a week ago," Mrs. Starflower replied. She was about to tell us more when she caught herself. I could tell she didn't feel comfortable being so candid with strangers.

Mr. Starflower smiled at us guardedly. "I don't believe we've had the pleasure of meeting you young people."

We introduced ourselves and explained how we knew Sasha. I asked, "Was Sasha upset after she and Nick broke up?"

Uh-oh. Maybe that question came a little too fast. Mrs. Starflower seemed taken aback. Her face grew rigid, and her husband frowned, his friendly manner turning formal. Sometimes I forget that what *I* call curiosity others call nosiness.

Bess shot me a look that said, *Let me handle things from here, Drew.*

"Mrs. Starflower," she said, "Nancy is a famous detective back home. Don't mind her. She's always asking questions like that. She can help."

Mrs. Starflower smiled hesitantly, and I grinned back. She let down her guard. "Sasha *had* seemed quite troubled lately," she told us. "I assumed it was because of her breakup with Nick. Before that happened, she was always cheerful."

"Nick seemed upset by it too," Ned observed.

Glancing at the Starflowers, I added, "Was the breakup mutual?"

Again they seemed a bit put off by my curiosity. But Mr. Starflower recovered quickly. "It was Sasha's idea," he said. "Still, she was sad. They'd been together for six months, and she really liked him."

"Then why did she break up with him?" I asked.

"I never asked—I didn't wish to pry," Mr. Starflower said coolly.

I paused. Was he giving me a hint? But his next question took me by surprise. "Nancy, you're a detective. How about investigating Sasha's disappearance? I'm sure there's more to it than meets the eye."

I was flattered. Who wouldn't be? I was a stranger, yet he trusted me to find his daughter. Still, I wasn't sure I agreed with him that there was anything more to her disappearance. She was probably not a crime victim, but simply lost.

"Nick has been acting so strangely," he went on. "You kids saw him. Now tell me, is that behavior normal? I'm just really worried that he might have something to do with Sasha being gone."

I sighed. I didn't want to disappoint him by telling him my opinion. "I agree that Nick was acting weird," I said, choosing my words carefully. "And he may be hiding something. But that doesn't prove he's responsible for a serious crime."

Mr. Starflower frowned. "The more I think about Nick, the more suspicious he seems. After they broke up, Sasha complained that Nick wouldn't leave her alone. Almost as if he was stalking her."

"You both mentioned that Nick isn't honest," I said. "Can you be more specific?"

Mrs. Starflower's delicate fingers brushed nervously over her hair. She reminded me of a ballet dancer, with her gracefulness and her proud straight posture. "Sometimes he would date other girls," she said. "Not seriously, but he'd keep that part of his life from Sasha. She'd find out from mutual friends, and when she asked him about it, he'd say nothing. Yet he was always pestering her for more of a commitment. His neediness and lack of honesty drove her away from him."

"He was upset enough by the breakup to want revenge," Mr. Starflower said, "even though he never came right out and said that."

A knot of dread thickened in my stomach. Was he voicing something I'd been wondering myself? My mind flashed back to last night. Nick got so touchy when we mentioned the dirt on his shirt at the Laughing Tortilla. His manner was evasive—and suspicious. Still, I had to be the voice of reason with Mr. Starflower, who seemed so sure of Nick's guilt.

"There's no evidence that Nick was involved in Sasha's disappearance," I said, "only a hunch. All the evidence points to Sasha being lost."

"Nancy, I disagree," Mr. Starflower said. "Sasha has superior tracking abilities—I taught her those skills myself when she was a tiny girl. There's no way she just got lost."

My friends nodded gravely. "He's right," George said. "Remember yesterday in Arches when Bess fainted? Sasha was very cool. She knew exactly what to do. The desert is like her home."

"I can't imagine Sasha being lost for this long," Ned said. "I mean, she's a guide and a park ranger."

"I'm surprised she's still lost too," I said. "I just think we need more evidence before we jump to conclusions that there's been foul play. But I'd be glad to take on the case. If more evidence exists, I'll do my best to find it."

The Starflowers beamed. "Oh, thank you, Nancy," Mrs. Starflower said, blinking back tears. "You've given us hope."

I assured the ranger that my investigation wouldn't get in the way of his. I also asked him to let me know if he found any clues, and vice versa. We said good-bye, and I promised the Starflowers I'd be in touch soon.

Just before leaving, I remembered an important question. "Where had Sasha been living?" I asked her parents, thinking I might look for clues there.

"At a luxurious dude ranch outside Moab called Red Horse Ranch," Mrs. Starflower said. "She is taking care of the horses in exchange for room and board."

With that information, an idea started bubbling in my head. On our way back to Moab, I suggested to my friends that I move over to Red Horse for a couple days to cast a wider net in the investigation. Bess, liking the word *luxurious,* offered to come with me, while George and Ned decided to stay at the Ranger Rose to keep an eye on Nick. A quick phone call on our return sealed the reservation. The owner of Red Horse, a jolly older man named Earl Haskins, even offered to lend us his extra Jeep.

Later that afternoon George and Ned dropped us off at Red Horse. Once we were settled, Bess and I explored the gorgeous grounds. Simple, well-made cabins dotted the green lawns that were shaded by cottonwoods and stately pines. Large horse pastures surrounded the buildings. On one side the view was of snow-covered mountains. On the other we could see red-rock canyons and desert mesas. A main building housed a comfortable lobby and a rustic dining room with an elk's head overlooking a cheerful fireplace.

"Let's check out the game room, Nan," Bess suggested, noticing a sign for it pointing right. "I'll challenge you to a game of pool."

She led the way—then stopped dead in her tracks. The pool table was already taken, by none other than Missy Powell.

A spark of blue flashed on Missy's finger as she shot the cue. I gasped. Missy was wearing Sasha's turquoise ring!

6

Avalanche

Isn't that Sasha's ring?" Bess exclaimed, always alert to fashion.

Missy smiled as she fingered its smooth turquoise surface. "Lovely, isn't it?"

"How did you get it?" Bess asked. "I mean, I doubt Sasha gave it to you. It was a birthday present from her father."

"Is that so?" Missy said vaguely. "Well, Sasha *did* give it to me, at least temporarily." She lined up another shot, her blue eyes squinting like a hawk gauging prey. With a loud crack, the orange ball rolled into a pocket.

"You'd better tell us how you got the ring," I said, "unless you want us to suspect you of stealing it."

Missy waved her hand. "I don't care what you

girls think. But if you must be so nosy, I'll tell all. When we were hiking in Canyonlands yesterday, I noticed the ring. I told Sasha how beautiful it was, so she let me try it on. Sasha got lost before she had a chance to take it back, so now it's temporarily mine."

Bess and I traded looks. I decided not to get into awkward details with Missy for now—that she was not related to Sasha, so had no claim to her ring.

Looking at Missy, Bess asked, "Are you staying here too?"

"Sure am," Missy said, shooting the yellow ball into a pocket.

"What was wrong with the Ranger Rose?" I asked, even though her answer wasn't hard to guess.

"Mom. She's just so embarrassing," Missy replied. "I couldn't stand being with her a moment longer. Plus, the Ranger Rose is such a dump. At least there's a decent spa here, and the horseback riding is okay."

"But . . . aren't your mom's feelings hurt?" Bess asked.

Missy shrugged. "She barely notices—too busy meditating. Anyway, I'm here now, so I might as well make the best of it." She flashed us a friendly smile. "Want to play pool?"

"Not now," I said, elbowing Bess. "Maybe after we unpack. But thanks anyway."

Back in our cabin, I sat on my incredibly comfortable brass bed across from Bess's. I wanted to discuss the case with Bess right away—especially this new Missy angle.

"I think we should keep an eye on Missy," Bess said firmly. "She and her mom were the last to see Sasha, and Missy is wearing her ring! She might as well have the word *guilt* written across her chest."

"But why would the Powells want to ditch Sasha in the desert?" I countered. "Nick makes more sense as a suspect. He was Sasha's ex-boyfriend, he was upset when they broke up, and he might want revenge."

Bess frowned. "I just have a hunch that Nick's not guilty."

"But we've got to look at the evidence, too," I said. "It's true, the Powells don't seem very sorry about Sasha. That's pretty weird. Are they really just selfish, though, or is there something else going on?"

"Maybe Sasha fell and hurt herself, and the Powells didn't want to deal with helping her back to safety," Bess suggested. "Then they panicked about being held responsible for abandoning her, so they lied and said she left them, making it seem like her fault.

And Missy's fine with that, she's got Sasha's ring."

I had to admit Bess was on to something. The ring was our first real clue. "Nick had motive, and the Powells had opportunity," I told Bess. "I've got to consider them both."

"This food tastes great!" George exclaimed, biting into her grilled chicken with lime juice and chili peppers. "Hot, though," she added, reaching for a sip of iced tea.

"It's real Southwestern fare," Mrs. Starflower said. "Hot, spicy, and heavily grilled, with a Mexican influence. A lot of local ingredients are used, like corn and peppers."

The Starflowers had invited my friends and me that evening to join them at this fancy Moab restaurant that served Southwestern grilled dishes. I think they appreciated my helping them look for Sasha. Dining with us was a friend of Mrs. Starflower's, Nigel Brown, a British archaeologist who specialized in ancient Indian civilizations. He explained that the name *Anasazi* meant "Ancient Ones" in the Navajo language.

"The Anasazi were fascinating," he said, his green eyes looking lost in thoughts of ancient times. "They had an advanced civilization. They lived in these intricate cliff dwellings in Utah, New Mexico, Arizona, and Colorado. Of course, those weren't states back then."

"I heard that the Anasazi packed up and left overnight around thirteen hundred A.D.," I said, remembering what Sasha had told us yesterday in Arches. "Is it true that no one knows why?"

Mr. Brown smiled pleasantly. "Unfortunately, it's true. I wish I knew why they left, Nancy. But I'm currently on a dig in Arizona looking for clues to Anasazi culture. My bet is—and a lot of archaeologists agree with me—that the Hopi Indians are direct descendants of the Anasazi."

Ned tilted his head. "I've read about the Hopi. They live in Arizona, right?" he asked.

Mr. Brown nodded. "They live in pueblos, which are community buildings made of stone or adobe, similar to the Anasazi cliff dwellings. They're a fascinating tribe. Their family line descends through the mother instead of the father, and they're known for being very private, but very peaceful. The name *Hopi* means 'Peaceful Ones.'"

"You certainly know a lot!" Bess exclaimed.

"No more than Kate does," Mr. Brown said, glancing at Mrs. Starflower.

"Nigel is way too modest," Mrs. Starflower told us.

"He's a leading authority in England on the ancient American Southwest. But I haven't cracked a book about it since he and I were archaeology students together at Oxford years ago."

"You studied the Southwest in college?" George asked her.

"That's how I met Paul—on a student dig in Arizona," Mrs. Starflower explained with a fond glance at her husband. "I returned to live here after getting my degree, and Nigel always enjoys visiting old friends when he's in the neighborhood." She paused, casting her eyes downward, as if suddenly remembering a painful thought.

I knew that Sasha was never far from her mind. Just as Sasha was never far from mine.

"You're really going riding with Missy?" Bess asked me after breakfast the next morning. She looked horrified. "You'll be stuck with her alone for at least two hours."

"A perfect opportunity for me to question her about Sasha," I said. "It's a good thing Red Horse has a rule against riding alone. Otherwise, Missy never would have asked me to come with her. I'm not exactly her favorite person."

"Who is?" Bess said. "Anyway, at least she won't be able to dodge your questions out on the trail." She paused for a moment. "Guess what I'm doing this morning, Nancy? Helping Nick repair bikes at the Cliff-Hanger, this rental shop where he works part time."

I grinned. Maybe Bess didn't look the part, but she was actually a wiz mechanic. "Awesome, Bess. Maybe you'll discover some clues linking him to Sasha's disappearance."

"Maybe I'll learn enough to prove him innocent!" Bess said with a flick of her long blond hair. "But don't worry, Nancy. If Nick is guilty, I won't let him blind me to that. You know I'll do whatever I can to find Sasha."

An hour later Missy and I were riding into the hills on a path that wound through a fragrant pine grove. Moon Dance, my horse, was a beautiful dappled gray with a gentle temper. Missy's horse, Cricket, a lively black mare, led the way. The sun beat down, and I could tell the mercury was heading way past ninety degrees. Another scorcher. But the scrub firs gave us some shade, and the heat actually brought out their great pine smell. The higher we climbed, the better the view of desert cliffs in shades of orange and red, rimmed by snowy mountains.

I pulled up beside Missy to ask her some questions. After all, I wasn't there just for the view.

"So, Missy, what were you and your mom doing in Canyonlands before Sasha disappeared?" I asked, trying to sound unconcerned.

Missy whirled toward me, her face like an angry cloud. "None of your busi—"

A rumbling sound on the hill above us drowned out her words. I looked up. A rock avalanche was hurtling toward us—a tidal wave of giant boulders!

7

Mystery Woman

We didn't have a second to spare. Ahead of us, the trail passed under an overhanging cliff. Maybe the cliff would offer some shelter. It was our only hope.

Urging Moon Dance forward, I shouted to Missy to head straight for the cliff. But either she couldn't hear me over the deafening roar of the rocks, or she thought she had a better idea. Screaming in panic, she turned Cricket downhill in a hopeless attempt to outrun the avalanche.

I raced after her. The deadly cascade of rocks loomed over us. In seconds we would both be buried alive.

No time to waste words. I reached out, grabbed Cricket's bridle, and yanked her toward the overhang. We reached it in the nick of time. I could feel the hot rush of rocks brushing Moon Dance's tail.

The horses were terrified. Cricket reared up, flaying her legs and foaming at the mouth. Moon Dance's body shook uncontrollably, his eyes white and bulging. The avalanche sounded like a freight train as we huddled under the cliff, covering our ears. But the overhang did the trick—it totally sheltered us.

The landslide seemed to take hours, but it actually only lasted a minute. When the noise died down, I dismounted and gave Missy a comforting pat on the back. She stiffened away from me, then changed her mind and gave me a tentative smile. She was trembling harder than the horses. Her freckles stood out in a peppery mass against her sheet white face.

I leaned out from the overhang and cautiously peeked up at the mountain, alert to more rumbling sounds from above. But everything was quiet. We were safe!

Taking a deep breath, I scanned the hillside below. The landscape was freaky. Where scrub pines and dry grass had been minutes before, a field of rocks, all sizes and shapes, pocketed the slope. There was no evidence of trees. They'd been completely buried or uprooted. It was like a totally different place. But the trail ahead of us was clear.

"It's okay, Missy," I said. "The avalanche is over. Let's go." I knew I'd better make the decisions, or we'd be here all week. Missy was way too petrified to take action.

"Nancy, that was the scariest moment of my life," Missy said. Cricket, whinnying and prancing around, was a basket case. With a trembling hand, Missy tried to calm the skittish mare, but I think she made her more nervous. I stepped over to help.

After soothing Cricket and Moon Dance, I climbed onto Moon Dance and led the way forward. Missy said, "I hope you're not thinking of continuing on, Nancy. My nerves are way too shot. Let's get back to the ranch. An afternoon in the hot tub is my only hope for a cure."

"Okay," I said reluctantly. Rats. I was hoping to find out more about her hike with Sasha. I didn't have any more time to lead up to the conversation in a subtle way. I only hoped Missy wouldn't be too nervous to talk. There was only one way to find out. I plunged ahead. "So what were you and your mom and Sasha talking about before she disappeared?" I asked. "Do you remember?"

She shot me a puzzled look. "What made you think of Sasha, Nancy? How can you even talk about her when we were almost killed?"

"Because she's in danger too."

Missy frowned. "I can't possibly think of anything but how traumatized I am," she complained. "I mean, my brain is totally shaken. You lead back please, Nancy. But absolutely no talking. I can't deal with it."

I couldn't help but roll my eyes—and fortunately Missy was too preoccupied with her own stress to notice. Twenty minutes later we were handing the horses over to a groom at Red Horse. We told him about the avalanche and that the horses needed to spend a stress-free afternoon.

After he assured us he'd pamper the horses, Missy and I headed toward the main building, where a small spa was located behind the dining room in one of the wings. Missy seemed shell-shocked—too stressed to talk. "A massage first, then a long soak in the hot tub," she muttered as we crossed the lobby. She turned down the hall to the spa, moving like a zombie.

My heart sank. With no information from Missy, my morning had been wasted. I now had no more clues on the case than I'd had last night. But I'm not my father's daughter for nothing. I immediately put my negotiating skills to the test.

Scooting in front of the doorway marked SPA, I blocked Missy's way. "I pulled you to safety under that cliff, Missy," I said firmly. "Now I want you to do something for me."

"What?"

"Draw me a map that shows the place where you last saw Sasha."

She crinkled her nose. "But my mother already told the police where we last saw her."

"I know, but a map would be helpful," I said. "It can't hurt."

She shrugged, too tired to make a fuss. "Okay, why not." Shoving me aside, she opened the spa door. A pungent herbal aroma greeted us. Once inside, Missy seemed to come alive. I had a hard time getting her to focus on the map with all the distracting lotions and tonics in colorful bottles on display shelves. But before long, she borrowed a pen and paper from the spa receptionist and drew me a crude map.

"Here, Nancy," she said, handing it to me. "Have a ball."

I left feeling perplexed. Sometimes Missy seemed totally heartless. But that didn't prove she'd actually harmed Sasha. Or even that she knew what had happened to her. I glanced at the map. It showed the Colorado River flowing just a mile away from where Sasha had last been seen. But if Missy or her mom were culprits, the map might be totally wrong. Missy might have deliberately drawn errors on it to mislead me. I gritted my teeth. I had no choice. The map was all I had to go on.

As I passed the front desk I ran into Earl Haskins, the owner of Red Horse Ranch. He was a gregarious man with curly gray hair and apple cheeks—and he didn't look busy.

"Mr. Haskins, could I ask you a few questions about Sasha?" I asked.

"Sure!" he said, eager to talk. "I know she's gone missing in Canyonlands; the police came by yesterday looking for information. How can I help you, young lady?"

"Sasha was working here, taking care of the horses for room and board," I said. "Was there anything unusual that happened while she was here?"

Mr. Haskins frowned. "Unusual? Yes, I reckon so. See, she worked here until last week. Then she suddenly quit. She never gave me a good reason why. But I liked the girl, so I told her she could take her time looking for a new place to live."

"Hmm. Well, did she act any differently from her normal self around the time she quit?"

"She sure did," he said, puffing out his fleshy cheeks. "She went from being a cheerful, talkative girl to a sad one. Something was bugging her, I just know it."

I perked up. "Do you have any clue what?"

"I reckon so," he said. He picked up a pen and chewed it thoughtfully. "Sasha's good-for-nothing boyfriend had been lurking around, and she wanted

64

independence from him. So she broke up with him. Don't blame her a bit. He'd been getting on her nerves, and she thought she'd be happier without him. They broke up a day or so before she quit."

"It sounds like she wanted a total change in her life," I said.

Mr. Haskins shrugged. "I thought she'd be happier after the breakup, but the opposite happened. I'm guessing she quit here because she was so sad. Still, I don't get it. Why wasn't she thrilled she'd finally dumped the lout?" He sighed, throwing out his hands. "Who can explain love?" he said philosophically. "You can't understand people unless you're in their shoes."

I thought for a moment. So Sasha had been sad about Nick. He must have meant something to her despite her wish to break up with him. I wasn't sure whether this information helped me in my search for her. Only time would tell.

I was about to thank Mr. Haskins for his time, when his face suddenly brightened.

"Nancy," he said, clearing his throat, "there's one more thing about Sasha that you ought to know."

I was all ears.

Mr. Haskins pursed his lips, looking thoughtfully at a woven Indian basket he displayed on a side table.

Finally he spoke. "In the last month or so, Sasha had grown very interested in the ancient Anasazi people. Do you know who they were?"

"Yes, Sasha told me about them," I replied. "When we met her, she was photographing their cliff drawings in Arches."

"She did that a lot," Mr. Haskins mused. "She also bought books and surfed the Internet to learn whatever she could."

"Do you know what suddenly made her interested in them?" I asked.

"Oh, I don't know if I can point to a particular thing," he told me. "I think it was a general curiosity that developed over time. But she only started talking about the Anasazi in the last month or so."

"What would she say?" I asked.

"That their mysterious history intrigued her, and how advanced their cliff dwellings were," he said. "She also admired their petroglyphs and pottery. Sometimes, she'd visit Anasazi ruins, like Mesa Verde in Colorado and Chaco Canyon in New Mexico. She'd take long car drives just to view them. I think she enjoyed imagining what it was like to be there in thirteen hundred A.D. and trying to guess what had happened to them." He shook his head. "The Anasazi vanished out of the blue. It's as if aliens came down one day and swept them off the Earth."

"Did Sasha take these trips alone?"

"Sometimes Nick went with her, but mostly she went alone," he said. "Though she often spoke about Andy Littlewolf. He's a Navajo dealer in antiquities. He might have gone with her sometimes. You might try talking to him."

Andy Littlewolf. The name rang a bell. Hadn't Sasha mentioned him to us? "Where can I find him?" I asked.

"He has an antique shop in Moab called Little-wolf's," Mr. Haskins told me. "It's long drive from his reservation, so he only works there three days a week. In fact, just this morning I visited the shop, looking for knickknacks to spruce up this lobby. So I know Andy's in. He was whispering in a corner with some gray-haired woman in patched jeans and a tie-dyed shirt, a weird-looking gal." He snorted. "Believe me, you get the strangest types here in Moab, Nancy."

8

Dangerous Waters

I **didn't wait around.** After asking Earl where I could find Mr. Littlewolf's store, I left the ranch in his Jeep.

Ten minutes later I pulled in front of Littlewolf's Antiques, two blocks away from the Ranger Rose on Main Street. I knew Margaret Powell wouldn't be there anymore, since Earl Haskins had spotted her over two hours ago. In fact, the place was empty when I stepped inside, except for a man dusting some pots in a display case. Mr. Littlewolf, I presumed.

He was the opposite of Earl Haskins. Lean and tall with dark hair pulled into a long ponytail, Mr. Littlewolf greeted me with a curt nod. I introduced myself and waited several seconds for him to respond. Earl

Haskins would spill the beans on any subject, while Andy Littlewolf seemed hard pressed to say hello. I ignored his stony expression and forged ahead with my questions. The first thing I asked him was whether he knew Sasha.

He nodded guardedly. "Sure, I know Sasha. She grew up near my home. Now, can I help you find something to buy in my store?"

"To be honest, I came here to ask you about Sasha. You may have heard she disappeared two days ago in Canyonlands," I said.

"I heard that." He turned his back on me to dust more pots.

"I'm helping the rangers with the search," I said to his back. "We're trying to learn information from her friends. Any detail about her could be useful. Please tell me whatever you know."

"I know no more than you do," Mr. Littlewolf replied. "Since I'm not responsible for her disappearance, I don't see how information from me could help."

I stepped back in surprise. Why would he think I suspected him in her disappearance? I switched gears. There was no advantage in making him feel like he was on the defensive. Then he'd refuse to answer questions, and I might as well leave.

I softened my voice. "No one ever blamed you for

Sasha being missing. That thought didn't occur to me. Let me ask you about your store." Glancing around the medium-size room, I saw a number of tables displaying pottery, arrowheads, and jewelry. In a corner was another table with more pottery and some carved wooden tribal figurines in various sizes, wearing colorful painted clothing and feather headdresses. "You've got some beautiful stuff," I told him.

My tactic worked. Mr. Littlewolf warmed up immediately. "I'm glad you think so," he said with a glimmer of a smile. "Most Navajo sell their own crafts on the reservation, but I'm interested in branching out. I want to sell antiques that aren't necessarily Navajo."

I picked up a pottery shard and studied it. There was a drawing of a flute player on it, wearing a headdress. "This piece looks quite old," I commented.

"That fragment is ancient—over seven hundred years old. It's part of an Anasazi pot," he said. "That's a picture of Kokopelli, the wandering hunchbacked flute player and magician. The Anasazi believed he brought rain and fertility. See, my specialty is Native American antiques, particularly Anasazi artifacts. Of course, most of those are so old, it's difficult to find anything in one piece."

"Where do you get these pottery fragments?" I asked.

"Believe it or not, I've found some in my own backyard," he said. "My Hogan—that's a Navajo house—faces a canyon. I've found a number of these fragments there. Sometimes archaeologists buy them from me to study."

Speaking of studying, I took a good look at Mr. Littlewolf. Why was he so talkative about Anasazi artifacts, and so silent about Sasha?

He went on. "The Anasazi were talented potters. Plenty of Anasazi relics are still hidden in caves in remote parts of the Southwest. Unfortunately that can be a problem."

"What do you mean?" I asked.

His eyes narrowed. "Because they belong to Native American tribes. For instance, if a hiker finds a pot inside a cave, the hiker has to leave it there. Taking ancient artifacts from federal or Indian land is illegal. But the lands are so huge and unpopulated, we can't really guard them. There aren't going to be many witnesses to a theft in the middle of the empty desert."

I thought for a moment about the Anasazi. Their mysteriousness was intriguing. "So what do you think made the Anasazi suddenly disappear?" I asked.

Mr. Littlewolf sighed. "I wish I knew. Some people think an astroid hit the area. Almost any theory is possible. There were thirty years of drought in the late thirteenth century around here. That must have strained the people's resources terribly."

"So you think they just went in search of more water?" I asked.

"Maybe," he said with a shrug. "Wouldn't you?"

"So you took these artifacts from your land to sell?" I asked.

"I'm a Native American. I can sell them," he said. "Of course, I would never do that if there was any hint they were from a sacred area. But the Anasazi aren't the only tribe whose artifacts interest me. I also like antique Navajo crafts and jewelry, as well as Hopi kachinas and pots."

"What are kachinas?" I asked.

"I see I have to give you a crash course on Southwestern Indian culture," he said pompously. He strode to the table where the carved wooden figures lay and held one up. It was about a foot high, and was intricately carved. It wore a red skirt, and feathers were glued delicately to five points on the headdress.

"This is a kachina, Nancy," he said. "It's a carved totemic figure that represents a particular spirit. There are many spirits in Hopi mythology who do both good and bad. I find Hopi legends fascinating. The Hopi are very private about their religion. They perform ceremonial dances and rituals. I would suggest that you go see a dance, but they close most of them off to outsiders."

I fingered a pot that lay beside one of the kachina dolls. An abstract drawing of a graceful butterfly decorated it. "This pot is gorgeous," I exclaimed.

"Don't touch it! It's my favorite one," he said. "The Hopi are known for their beautiful pottery, as well as for their kachinas."

Mr. Littlewolf was an odd man. He seemed aloof, but when he was interested in lecturing you, there was no stopping him. But his tone wasn't kind; it was bossy and arrogant. I pressed on, determined to get some information from him on Sasha.

"You certainly know a lot about the Hopi tribe, and the Anasazi," I said. Maybe flattery would loosen him up.

He shot me a tight smile. "Yes, I do. And you might as well know that it's unusual for a Navajo to take an interest in the Hopi. Our tribes are not always on the best of terms because of land claim disputes. Still, we Navajo have adopted some Hopi skills, like pottery."

"How come you're so interested in them?" I asked.

He shrugged. "Don't know. How does anyone get interested in anything? I've always enjoyed Hopi myths, and I've been interested in how the Anasazi influenced Hopi culture. As you can see, even though I mainly sell antiques, I can't resist the occasional Hopi craft. This is my Hopi table," he added, patting the table we stood beside. "I'd like to buy from them more often, but as a Navajo, I don't always feel welcome on their land."

"That must be frustrating," I said. "You ought to consider hiring a third person who isn't related to either tribe to buy for you."

"I have," he said crisply, and left it at that. "Is there anything else I can help you with, Nancy?"

Mr. Littlewolf was like an encyclopedia of the Southwest. I asked him a few more questions about the Anasazi and learned that Moab sat on the ruins of an eleventh and twelfth century pueblo farming community. The villages had been burned when the Anasazi left, and the ruins were scattered throughout the area. Mr. Littlewolf told me that corn was their big food staple, and that in addition to pots, the Anasazi made beautiful baskets.

"But the most amazing thing about them was their stone houses," he added. "They were built into cliffs and were really advanced. They even had sophisticated ventilation systems."

I tapped my foot. This information was interesting, but how would it help me find Sasha? Maybe telling me all this had relaxed Mr. Littlewolf enough to talk about her. No harm in pressing him again. "I hear Sasha was interested in the Anasazi," I began.

He immediately clammed up, his lips tightening into a scowl. I sighed. Obviously I wasn't getting anywhere with questions about Sasha. Once more I shifted gears. "Did a gray-haired woman come into your store this morning? I think she was wearing patched blue jeans."

Mr. Littlewolf's dark eyes flashed with anger. "I don't know what you're talking about. Now, if you don't mind, I have work to do." And he turned his back on me, flicking his ponytail over his shoulder in a dismissive gesture.

"Well, thanks for telling me about the Southwestern Indian tribes," I said.

"We didn't discuss nearly all of them," he said before shuffling into a back room marked PRIVATE.

Clearly there was nothing more for me to do here. I decided to walk to the Ranger Rose and make contact with George and Ned. Maybe they'd discovered some interesting info about Nick. At the very least, they might want to follow Missy's map into Canyonlands with me.

On the stoop of the Ranger Rose, I bumped into them coming out the door, dressed in shorts, T-shirts, and baseball hats. "Guess I just caught you," I said. "Are you guys heading some place exciting?"

"We set up this rafting trip on the Colorado River," Ned said. "I tried calling you over at Red Horse, but Mr. Haskins told me you'd left already. I'm really glad we ran into you." He flashed me a smile.

"Me too," I said, grinning. "So did you learn anything more about Nick?"

George shrugged. "Last night Ned and I had a soda with him after getting back from dinner with the Starflowers. We hung out at that burger place where we ate our first night in Moab, remember? I didn't notice anything suspicious about him. Did you, Ned?"

"Nope," Ned said. "He joked around with some customers he knew. He mainly spoke about biking. He never even mentioned Sasha or his behavior yesterday in front of her parents. It's like he has two personalities or something."

"Did you see him today?" I asked.

"No," George said. "He's working."

"Oh, yes," I said, remembering. "At the Cliff-Hanger with Bess."

"So do you want to go rafting, Nancy?" Ned asked me eagerly. "River Outfitters is just a few blocks down the street. They already have a guide and a raft reserved for us."

I hesitated. "I'd like to, except I'd been hoping you guys would help me find the place where the Powells last saw Sasha. Missy made a map for me and marked it with a red X." I dug the map from my pocket and showed it to my friends.

George pointed to the blue squiggle indicating the Colorado River. "Missy drew the river flowing close to that spot," George said. "Maybe we could raft part of the way and hike inland."

"Awesome idea, George," I said. "I hope our guide won't mind leading us there. Before we go, I want to call the Starflowers to update them on the case. I'll let them know we're on our way to Canyonlands by way of Missy's map."

Mr. Starflower was grateful for my call and wished me luck. On the way to River Outfitters, I filled in Ned and George on my meeting with Mr. Littlewolf, and the fact that Earl Haskins had spotted a woman who was probably Margaret in Mr. Littlewolf's shop earlier.

Once there, we were greeted by our guide, a young guy named Byron. After introducing ourselves, we spread Missy's map on the shop counter and asked Byron if he could take us to the place marked X. After a moment studying the map, he pushed back his mop of blond hair and said, "Sure! If this map is right, I know a trail that leads between the river and the X. It's only about a mile inland. For a small extra fee, I can guide you all there."

I chewed my lip. I didn't have much confidence in Missy's map-drawing abilities. I also realized she could have deliberately made errors on it to lead us astray. At the same time, I knew that the map could be right. If so, the Powells probably followed the trail back to the river, then hiked to safety along the bank. Otherwise, how could two amateur hikers have found their way out of Canyonlands in the dark?

But if the Powells could find the trail that led to the river, then why couldn't Sasha—unless she'd been prevented? My heart beat faster. Something must have trapped or injured her, so she couldn't find the trail. Something human, or animal. Like Sasha's father, I couldn't believe she'd just gotten lost.

About half an hour later Byron, George, Ned, and I climbed into a yellow inflatable raft that had sides about a foot high. We wore life jackets over our T-shirts.

"Here, guys, each of you take a paddle," Byron said, tossing them to us. "I may need your help to get us through the rapids. They can be fierce."

"I guess that big storm the other day made the river pretty high," I said.

Byron grinned. "Sure did. It's a lot of fun, though. We won't be going through really tough white water—I don't take first timers out in that. Still, we'll see some challenging stuff, so make sure your life vests are tight."

We helped Byron put a large waterproof box into the boat. It was filled with extra water, food, and first aid supplies. "Other than the water and chocolate chip cookies, we rarely use this stuff," he assured us. "Still, better to be safe than sorry."

Soon we were spinning down the river toward Canyonlands, surrounded by tall red cliffs. The afternoon sun blasted us, and there was absolutely no shade. The deep blue sky radiated heat. I dipped my paddle into the water, which was a chalky rust color from desert runoff.

We took turns paddling, but otherwise slathered on sunscreen, sat back, and relaxed.

"So where are the big rapids?" George asked Byron as she sipped water from her canteen. "This river is so lazy we're hardly moving."

"Honey, you haven't seen what this river can do," Byron said, cracking a smile. "Appearances are deceiving. Be glad for the calm before the storm."

But the current was so slow and the heat so intense that I felt sleepy. Ned, though, had a perfect cure for that. "I'm going swimming," he announced. "Want to come?" Without waiting for an answer, he threw off his sandals, hat, and sunglasses and jumped into the water, clothes and all. "The water feels great. Jump in!"

George and I needed no persuading. Making sure that my life jacket was secure, I slid off the side of the raft into the chalky water. It may not have looked inviting, but no swim had ever felt so cool and refreshing. Byron slowed the raft with his paddle so we could keep up. But after a few minutes, the raft swept ahead.

Byron shot us a warning look. "Get back in the boat, ASAP. Rapids ahead. Swimmers beware."

Ned, George, and I swam next to the raft while Byron stalled it with his paddle. He reached down to help me over the side. But as I gripped it, the rubber felt strange to me—flimsy.

"Hey!" Byron shouted, his face paling despite his tan. "There's a huge rip in the side of the raft. It's deflating!"

The current grew stronger, pulling us along. Byron and the waterproof box were leaning toward the water. In seconds, they'd plunge in with us.

I glanced toward the rapids. Large jagged rocks pointed upward, with tiny fierce waves slapping around them. The current tugged harder, sweeping us along.

9

Ancient Artifacts

Grab the raft and hold on!" Byron shouted as he fought to keep it steady. Luckily the three of us were still bobbing next to the raft. We took hold of it, but it was way too wobbly to do us much good. I knew our weight would pull it over in no time.

"Let's try to push this thing to shore," I yelled to Ned and George. "At least it's something to cling to."

"Don't lean too hard," Ned warned. "The air is going out fast."

The three of us kicked like crazy, hoping to reach the riverbank ahead of the current. Byron paddled as hard as he could before the raft deflated any more. I peeked over the brim. The bank was still twenty feet away. My heart raced. I hadn't realized how wide the river was.

Using every ounce of energy, the four of us kicked and pushed and paddled. Byron's arm muscles strained, and Ned, George, and I choked on water that slapped our faces as the flow swept us along.

"Faster!" I shouted. The raft surged ahead as we kicked together in a burst of determination. I kicked harder and harder until my foot hit an underwater rock.

Pain shot through me. For a moment I felt paralyzed. I hung in the water, dizzy from the impact. My whole leg throbbed. If the white water rocks were as sharp as that one, we'd be sliced apart in ten seconds flat.

Suddenly something was pulling me. The current! I forced myself to stay alert.

Adrenaline surged through me. We had to reach the bank. "Ten more yards!" Byron yelled. "Kick, everyone—keep pushing!" But the current was getting stronger.

Another rock grazed my knee. I flinched.

"Ow!" Ned yelled. He raised his face from the water, a bright red spot spreading across his forehead. I could already see a bump rising there. I looked downstream. Just ahead, the rapids boiled. The waves were like tiny white flames lapping the air.

A whirlpool yawned at the brink of the rapids. Surrounded by rocks like giant's teeth, it looked ready to eat us alive.

I judged the distance between us and the rapids—about ten feet. We still had a chance. Making one more huge effort, I kicked off from the rock underneath me, held my breath, and pushed the raft.

We skimmed toward shore. The moment my feet touched the riverbed, a thrill of relief went through me. Traction! With the water too shallow for paddling, Byron rolled off the raft to help us push. We reached the bank. Safe at last.

I staggered to my feet. Standing in shallow water, we all stared at one another, dripping wet and gasping as if we'd just run a race.

"Hey, guys, let's get the raft onto land," Byron said.

We all pitched in and dragged it onto the shore. Fortunately the cliff here was set back, and a pebbly beach rose gradually from the riverbed.

The moment the raft was secure, we peeled off our life preservers and flopped to the ground, exhausted. I glanced over at Ned. Blood trickled down his face from his forehead cut.

"Let's get out the first aid kit," I said to Byron. "Ned cut his head on a rock."

Byron unstrapped the waterproof box and took out the kit. Everything still looked dry. He handed the kit to me, and I took out a gauze pad, some peroxide, and a bandage.

Ned winced as I gently cleaned his cut. I was

relieved to see that it wasn't that bad. "No big deal," I said, trying to cheer him up. After smoothing on the bandage, I added, "This will stop the bleeding in no time."

"Head wounds always bleed a lot," Ned said as I stooped next to him. "They look much worse than they really are."

"There's a bump, though," I said. "Do you have a headache?"

Ned smiled. "Nope. I promise I don't have a concussion, Nancy. By the way, you're an excellent nurse."

"Thanks, Ned. I just hope I won't have to practice my nursing skills any more on this vacation." I pulled my wet hair into a topknot, then scrambled for my hat, shoes, and sunglasses, which were safely tucked into the hull of the raft.

Ned lay on the shore for a few more seconds as he gathered his strength. Meanwhile Byron and I inspected the raft, which by now had almost completely deflated, and George sat on the beach munching trail mix.

"Weird! I wonder what caused this?" Byron said, peering at the rip in the side. "It couldn't have been cut by a rock—the gash is too high up."

"You're right. It's really strange," I said. "Could you have cut it by mistake without knowing?"

Byron chewed his lip, thinking. "I use a knife

sometimes to cut the anchor rope if the knot is too tight, but I don't think I used one recently. And I definitely would have noticed cutting the raft."

I walked around the raft, inspecting all the sides. "Hey, Byron, what's this?" I asked. I ran my finger over a thin piece of yellow tape near the gash.

Byron frowned as he studied the tape, which was only about three inches long. "I have no idea. I never patched this raft. This is news to me, for sure."

"The tape blends in perfectly with the yellow rubber," I observed. "I only noticed it because I was on the lookout for clues about what caused the rip."

Byron cocked his head and studied me. "What, are you a detective or something, Nancy? I mean, you're really observant. I'm impressed."

I laughed. I hadn't realized I was *that* obvious. But I had to keep my detective work a secret from some if I hoped to discover any secrets in Moab. "Uh, I'm interested in figuring out simple mysteries, like what caused our raft to rip," I mumbled.

"Have you got any theories?" Byron asked.

"Not yet. Can I take off this tape?"

Byron nodded, and I peeled it back. Underneath was another slit, much smaller and more evenly cut. "This doesn't look accidental," I said. "Look how neat it is."

Byron's green eyes widened. "That's bizarre," he

muttered. "Why would anyone cut a hole in the raft?"

I studied the rubber between the two slits. A small bump caught my eye. "What in the world?" I said. I reached inside and felt a hard metal object.

It was a small penknife. Its chrome blade gleamed in the sunlight as I held the tiny hilt. I touched the point. Sharp as a razor.

"Whoa, Nancy, that is freaky," Byron said. "How did a knife get in there?"

"I don't know," I replied. "But I'm sure it was done on purpose." I thought for a moment. Different scenarios of what might have happened flashed through my brain. But no matter how hard I tried to come up with other explanations, a sabotage theory made the most sense.

Ned and George wandered over to us, drawn by our surprised voices. After telling them about the penknife, I explained my theory.

"I think someone deliberately tried to sink our raft," I said grimly. "Probably the person made a small slit with the knife, then placed the knife inside the rubber, and taped over the gash before the rubber deflated."

George nodded. "As long as the raft was inflated, no one would notice the knife. There'd be so much air around it."

I added, "The person probably guessed that the rapids would make the knife poke a hole in the rubber from the inside. It probably wouldn't have happened in the calm section of the river."

"But who knew we were going rafting?" Ned asked. "I don't think I mentioned our plans to anyone except the desk clerk."

"Me neither," George said. "Let's think, though. Ned, you and I decided at breakfast to go rafting, and we asked the desk clerk for information. He told us about River Outfitters, and we called and spoke to you, Byron." Her dark eyes studied Byron's boyish face.

"I was the only person on duty when you guys called," Byron said. "The other river guides were already on the river with customers who had pre-reserved rafts. The only reason I could take you all spur-of-the-moment is that we got a cancellation. Believe me, I didn't tell anyone about our trip. I just filed a memo in the office log, as a standard safety measure in case we didn't come back."

"I totally believe you, Byron," I said, "but even if you *had* mentioned our trip, you didn't do the wrong thing. We're just trying to figure out who could have done this."

"I know," he said. "Any other thoughts?"

I turned to George and Ned. "What about Margaret

or Nick? Did you see them this morning?"

"They weren't around," George said, "and Bess was at Red Horse with you, Nancy. Really, the only person we mentioned this to was the desk clerk."

Ned glanced at me, a lock of hair covering his bandage. His brown eyes were clear and alert—showing, to my relief, no sign of a concussion. "Did you tell Bess where we were going?" he asked me. "She could have mentioned it to someone."

"She could have mentioned it to Nick at the Cliff-Hanger today," I said, "except I know I didn't tell her. I didn't even realize we were going rafting till I ran into you guys at the Ranger Rose." I paused, thinking. "Hey, Ned, remember how you phoned Red Horse this morning looking for me? Did you let Earl Haskins know your plans?"

Ned shook his head. "I just asked for you, and Earl said you were on your way into Moab. I thanked him. End of conversation. I definitely never mentioned rafting to him—why would I?"

I cast my mind back to every conversation I'd had today. I'd talked with Mr. Littlewolf, of course, but I hadn't known I was going rafting then.

My conversation with Mr. Starflower flashed through my mind. "Wait!" I said. "Remember just before we headed out, I called the Starflowers to update them on the case? I told Mr. Starflower where we were going. He said he hoped we'd find Sasha—or at least some evidence of where she is. He also said he was on his way to Littlewolf's Antiques to ask Mr. Littlewolf questions about Sasha. Mr. Starflower knew those two were friends."

"Do you think he could have told Mr. Littlewolf about our rafting trip?" Ned wondered.

"Possibly," I said. "I can ask him when we get back. But if Mr. Littlewolf knew, then he could have told Margaret about it—that is, if she returned to his shop. There's a whole possible chain of events here."

"You've lost me, guys," Byron said, looking confused. "I guess the point is that somehow, someone knew you were out on the river and meant to hurt you. Not a good scene at all."

There was no arguing with that. As we packed supplies for our hike inland, I pocketed the penknife for evidence. Also, as a tool, it might come in handy. After all, this was Canyonlands—a major desert wilderness.

"Everybody ready?" Byron asked, hoisting a small backpack and adjusting his dark glasses. "Let's head downriver. Fortunately the trail inland isn't far away."

We followed him down the beach, past an awesome stretch of white water. We were lucky to get out of the water when we did, or we'd have been diced fish food. From the shore, the rapids were beautiful as they swirled and foamed tirelessly over the rocks.

Soon we came to a trail leading away from the water, and I pulled out my trusty map. Missy had drawn a bend in the river, with a red rock arch marking the beginning of the trail. And there it was, ahead of us! I had to admit that Missy was not a bad cartographer—at least so far.

We made our way under the arch, which was the portal to a canyon filled with awesome rock formations. Byron said, "This part of the park reminds me of the Grand Canyon, except I think it's nicer. It doesn't have tons of tourists coming in, so it feels more remote. I really like that."

He pointed out some desert wildlife—a rabbit hopping through some brush, a small brown bird perched on a pine tree, and a rattlesnake. Fortunately, the snake was more than ten feet away, and the moment we heard its warning rattle, we quietly scooted off in the other direction.

"Look, everybody," Byron said about ten minutes later, "guess what these prints are?"

Ned, George, and I looked down at the place where he was pointing. Canine prints were pressed into the soft red dirt.

"Coyote," Byron said, and I felt a prickle of fear. Maybe Sasha had been hurt by a wild animal after all.

"I am so thirsty," George said, taking a swig of water from a bottle in her pack.

We all felt parched. Every now and then, we'd drink water and nibble on salted nuts. To take my mind off the heat, I studied the bands of color in the canyon walls.

"Why are they different colors?" I asked Byron.

"Each band is from a separate geological era millions of years old," he explained. "Oh, and look—there's a petroglyph." I glanced at the cliff face. There was a picture of a bison along with some human figures. "Let me check this place against the map," he added.

I handed it over. "So this is where the X is," he told us after a moment, gesturing at the surrounding area.

I peered across his shoulder at the map. He was right. Missy had drawn the X next to these petro-glyphs.

We began to search for clues—behind bushes, under stones, everywhere. But try as we might to find evidence of Sasha, we came up empty handed. Still, I knew that appearances could be deceiving.

"This is where Missy last *saw* Sasha," I said, "but Sasha was last *known* to be somewhere else, investigating noise." I studied the canyon wall. A thin trail snaked up one side, barely noticeable in the dry over-grown grass. Could Sasha have hiked up there to check out the noise?

I had to know.

"Be right back, guys," I said, moving toward the trail.

"What? Where are you going, Nancy?" Ned asked, alarmed.

"I'm re-creating Sasha's steps. I'm thinking she went up that path—it's the only way forward. But don't worry. I won't go out of earshot."

Ned and George know me too well to argue when I'm on a scent, so I struck out on the trail. It wasn't too steep. After a few twists and turns, it fizzled into scrub grass and rocks. But the cliff side ahead had an interesting indentation in it. A cave? I headed straight there to find out.

Sure enough, it was a shallow cave about five feet deep. A small boulder in the back looked out of place, as if a person had set it there.

I studied it curiously. That thing was hiding something, or my name wasn't Nancy Drew.

I pushed against the boulder. It rolled back easily to reveal a natural cupboard filled with broken pottery. But what really grabbed my attention was a piece of paper lying on the ground, half hidden by a chunk of clay. On it were typed words on letterhead.

I picked it up. Andy Littlewolf's name and address jumped out at me in bold black print.

10

Desert Tricks

I **picked up the** paper. Some of the words had faded, and about a third of the page was torn off, but I could get the gist. It was a letter from Mr. Littlewolf to a mystery person whose name must have been on the missing fragment. Mr. Littlewolf was describing a legend in Hopi mythology.

This legend is called "The Revenge of the Blue Corn Ear Maiden," and it goes like this: Once upon a time, Blue Corn Ear Maiden and Yellow Corn Ear Maiden were in love with the same man. Yellow Maiden turned her rival into a coyote, who was captured and taken to Spider Woman, a powerful spirit. Spider Woman turned the coyote back into Blue Maiden, and instructed her on how she could take revenge on Yellow Maiden. Blue Maiden returned to her village and pretended to be friendly to Yellow Maiden. They ground corn together and fetched water. Blue Maiden filled her vessel, which Spider Woman had given her, and the water glistened with magic rainbow colors. Yellow Maiden was curious, so she drank from it and instantly turned into a snake. From that time on, her life was filled with hardship. She was turned away by her own people, who thought she was just a snake.

The rest of the letter was a bunch of illegible ink stains, maybe from rain or dew, but I could make out the faded ending: "Yours truly, Andy."

I sighed. How could I learn who Mr. Littlewolf had written to? I studied the pottery fragments. All were broken. As my gaze roamed the cave, I couldn't help wondering whether Sasha had run into Mr. Littlewolf here. If so, could he have harmed her somehow? But why would he want to kidnap or hurt her? Maybe she'd surprised him as he was doing something illegal, like stealing artifacts.

I swigged some water, thinking. Would taking stuff from here be illegal for a Native American? I wasn't sure. Anyway, I could always ask Mr. Littlewolf who this note was for. I pocketed it with a sense of satisfaction. It was my first solid clue in the case. Somehow it hinted that Sasha had not fallen prey to a wild animal. Maybe the letter had been hers.

I scrambled back to the spot marked X, taking care not to fall off the side of the cliff in my eagerness to show everyone my clue. "Mr. Littlewolf's address is a rural route in Monument Valley," I said to Byron after everyone had peeked at the letter. "How far away is that?"

"It's a couple hours south of Moab on the Navajo reservation."

I exchanged looks with Ned and George. I didn't want to blurt out our plans to Byron, but my friends understood me perfectly—we were to be off to Monument Valley ASAP.

After a few more minutes scouting for signs of Sasha, we trudged back to the riverbank. Byron used his cell to phone a colleague to fetch us in another raft, and we were back in Moab by sunset. We thanked him, then contacted Bess at the Cliff-Hanger and told her to meet us at the Laughing Tortilla for supper.

When we were all settled in at our table, we briefed her on our day, then asked about hers.

"How can you three eat after you almost drowned?" Bess said, looking amazed. "I can't believe someone sabotaged your raft. Anyway, I know it wasn't Nick. He was with me all day." She paused to place her order of chicken tacos with the waiter, then went on. "There's no question in my mind that Nick is totally innocent."

George threw her a skeptical look. "No surprise there. He's cute and he likes you, so of course you think he's innocent."

"Unfair, George!" Bess protested. "If there were the slightest clue Nick was guilty, I'd admit it. I want to find Sasha as much as you guys do. But there's no evidence pointing to him. I mean, being her ex-boyfriend shouldn't be a crime."

I thought about Bess's words. I was inclined to agree with her. The evidence? She was with Nick all day. No way could he have sabotaged the raft. He never even knew our plans.

"You're wondering about the dirt on Nick's shirt," Bess added. "And why he had a meltdown over it. Well, I can explain that. Nick is sensitive about Sasha dumping him, so he feels slightly crazed when anyone mentions her."

George frowned. Sometimes she just isn't willing to cut her cousin any slack, and I could tell this was one of those times. "That still doesn't explain the dirt on his shirt. Nick went ballistic over that, when no one had mentioned Sasha," she said.

"Nick takes his hiking seriously, and he doesn't like to fall," Bess said. "Okay, maybe he has a bad temper. But he's no kidnapper." She looked at us pleadingly. "Look, guys, he's got a rock solid alibi for today: me! What more can you ask for?"

George opened her mouth to say something contrary when I cut in. Sometimes I have to redirect the cousins when their ribbing gets too serious. "Well, Bess, you'll be happy to know I agree with you," I said, smiling at her surprised face. "Everything you said sounds totally plausible to me."

Bess lit up. "I knew you'd see my point, Nancy," she said, throwing George a look of mock scorn.

"So let's forget Nick for now," Ned said. "What about the other suspects?"

"You mean Missy and Margaret?" Bess said. "They couldn't plan a crime if their lives depended on it! And why would they want to hurt Sasha, anyway?"

"As I mentioned before, they could have accidentally caused something bad to happen, and then panicked when Sasha was hurt, and now they're covering up," I said.

Bess nodded. "Possible. But did either of them know you went rafting?"

"Margaret could have learned through Andy Littlewolf," I said. "That is, if she came back to his store, and if Mr. Starflower mentioned our plans

97

to Littlewolf. I tried calling Mr. Starflower before dinner to ask if he'd told anyone, but there was no answer."

"That's a lot of *if*s," George said. She asked me to describe my conversation with Mr. Littlewolf again. "Mr. Littlewolf is looking like the prime suspect, if you ask me," she added after I'd finished. "He was friends with Sasha, he clammed up when you asked him about her, and Mr. Starflower might have mentioned the rafting trip to him. And then you found his letter where she was in Canyonlands last."

"But we don't know that he wrote it to Sasha," I countered.

"Still, it was *from* him, and that's what's important," George said.

I shrugged. It was also important who the letter was for, but George was right that Andy Littlewolf made a lot of sense as a prime suspect. "First thing tomorrow, let's drive to his house in Monument Valley and see what's up," I suggested. "If he's working at his store in Moab, we'll have a perfect chance to check out his house for clues."

"Just clues?" Bess said. "I'm hoping we'll find Sasha herself."

"I can't believe this landscape," George said as she steered the car over the parched desert plain on our way to Monument Valley. "It's fantastic." I had to agree. It was eleven in the morning, and we were the only car on the road. It was as if we'd entered an alternate universe where there were no people, just rocks. The weirdest kinds of rocks too—on plateaus and mesas stretching as far as the eye could see, in stunning shades of red, brown, and orange. Erosion had carved them into a zillion wild shapes more bizarre than the most imaginative man-made sculptures I'd ever seen.

Ned interrupted my thoughts with a practical question. "What if Littlewolf is at home?"

"When we stop for lunch, let's call his store and make sure he's there," I said. "But don't worry, Ned, I'll find a way to sneak in somehow, even if he's in his house."

Ned shot me a wry smile before pulling on a sweatshirt to ward off the freezing air-conditioning. "That's exactly what worries me, Nancy."

I grinned. I love Ned's concern, but let's face it—my curiosity often takes me to scary places. If mysteries didn't interest me, Ned's life would be a lot more relaxed. But if mysteries didn't interest me, I'd be a totally different person. And I'm guessing Ned would have a problem with that.

I was suddenly distracted by the sight of a rock on our left that looked exactly like a Mexican sombrero.

"I can see why this town coming up is called Mexican Hat," Bess said, scanning the map. "These rock shapes are hilarious."

"Monument Valley starts around Mexican Hat, doesn't it?" George asked. "I think that's what the map said when I studied it earlier. Anyway, I know we're pretty close."

Last night, getting ready for our trip, I read about Monument Valley in my guidebook. A number of Hollywood Westerns had been filmed there, especially John Wayne movies. There was a small museum at Gouldings, a hotel run by the Navajo, that told visitors all about the history of moviemaking in Monument Valley. But I doubted we'd have time to see it. Finding Sasha was our goal.

Ned checked his watch. "Hey, it's almost noon, and I'm getting pretty hungry. I don't want to search Littlewolf's house on an empty stomach."

"Let's stop for lunch at Gouldings," I suggested. "We have to get directions anyway to his house." I explained to my friends what Gouldings was—a Navajo-run hotel with a cafeteria, museum, and gift shop. Bess perked up at the word *shop*.

"I'm not hungry yet," Bess said with a sly expression. "I think I'll build up my appetite first by shopping. I can be quick. I'll check out the store while you guys get directions to Mr. Littlewolf's. Oh, and don't forget to call his store to make sure he's there, and not here."

We stepped inside the Gouldings building, high on a bluff that overlooked the craggy Navajo land. The views were amazing, and I felt as if I'd been there before—maybe from watching Westerns.

"Here's the gift shop," Bess said brightly. "Meet you in the café."

The phones were occupied, so we all joined Bess in the shop. I was mesmerized by all the cool Navajo crafts. I headed for the counter to check out the jewelry, then stopped in surprise.

A gray-haired woman in a long Mexican-style skirt was talking to the salesgirl.

I stopped in my tracks. Wasn't that Margaret Powell?

I came closer. It *was* Margaret, and she was holding up a turquoise ring for the salesgirl to examine. Sasha's.

"I'm interested in selling this ring," Margaret said. "How much will you take for it?"

11

Kidnapped

I elbowed George. "Do you see who I see?" I asked her.

"Yup," George said, looking shocked.

"I'm going to ask her about that ring." With Ned busy checking out arrowheads and Bess trying on moccasins, I approached the counter, followed by George.

"Hello, Margaret," I said. She spun around.

"Oh hello, Nancy, George," she said, nodding at us. She closed her hand around the ring to hide it. "Nice to see you both here. What brings you to Monument Valley?" She plastered a smile on her face, but I could tell she didn't mean it.

"I was just about to ask you the same thing, Margaret," I said.

"Well, I'm here on business, you see," Margaret said, lowering her eyes sheepishly.

"What do you have in your hand?" George piped up.

Margaret giggled. "Ah, nothing! As I said, I'm here on business."

"Margaret, you're holding Sasha's ring. I saw it," I said.

Her smile disappeared, and her fist sprang open. The turquoise stone shone in her palm. "What do you mean, 'Sasha's ring'?" she asked with a puzzled frown. She held the ring close to her face, as if staring at it might give a clue to the real owner. "What makes you think this is Sasha's?"

"Because I saw it on her finger the other day at Arches," I answered.

"You did?" Margaret said, fingering the beads on her necklace. "Well, I had no idea this ring was hers."

I looked at Margaret doubtfully. She was covered in silver and turquoise Navajo jewelry. It was hard for me to believe that she hadn't noticed Sasha wearing that ring. "You and Missy spent an afternoon with Sasha in Canyonlands. You must have noticed her ring."

"Uh, well, now that you mention it, Nancy, I do remember Sasha wearing something like it," Margaret said, holding the ring up to the window light.

"But how can you be sure it's the same one?"

I thought about Margaret's question. Of course I knew it was Sasha's ring. It was the same size, oval shape, and color, with the identical filigree pattern on its silver frame. Plus, Margaret's own daughter had been wearing it, and knew that it was Sasha's. "Margaret," I began, "I saw it on Sasha's finger. It's pretty eye catching. Definitely it's the same ring. But anyway, where did you get it?" I didn't want to reveal that I knew Missy had been wearing it. I wanted to test Margaret, to see if she would acknowledge that.

By now, Bess and Ned had wandered over. I waited, bursting with curiosity to hear if Margaret would tell me the truth. If Margaret lied about Missy having it, I would know I couldn't trust anything else she told me.

"Where did I get it?" Margaret repeated in her wispy voice. "Why, Missy gave it to me. She owes me money for all the horseback riding and spa treatments she's been doing at Red Horse Ranch."

Hmm. Honest so far.

"So she gave you the ring instead of money?" I asked.

"She had a cash flow problem," Margaret said. "Don't ask me why—her father gives her plenty of money. But anyway, she couldn't pay me back with cash, so she suggested I sell the ring."

"Did she tell you that it wasn't hers to sell?" George asked.

"Oh no," Margaret said gravely. "She said the ring was a gift from a Navajo friend, and it was probably worth a bundle of bucks. She said I was better off with the ring than with cash—that it was worth far more than the money she owed me. So here I am, trying to sell it."

"I think you'd better give the ring back to Sasha's parents," I told her. "It really belongs to them—that is, until Sasha comes back."

Margaret knit her brow. "Oh, do you think I should do that? Okay." Turning to the salesgirl, she apologized for bothering her over nothing. "I've changed my mind about the ring, sorry." She turned to leave, but I stopped her. I wasn't quite finished.

"You know that store called Littlewolf's Antiques?" I asked her.

"You mean the one in Moab near the Ranger Rose?" she said. "I was there yesterday."

"Yes, I . . . uh, noticed you there," I fudged. I didn't see a reason to mention that Earl Haskins had actually been the one to see her. Since she didn't know him, she might just get confused and not focus on my questions.

"You did?" she asked with a puzzled frown. "I didn't see you."

"Oh, I just popped in quickly. Everything looked too expensive. I'm sure you didn't notice me because you were talking to Mr. Littlewolf. Were you shopping too?"

"Not exactly," Margaret said. "I was trying to sell him this ring. Selling it to Andy would have been so much more convenient than coming down here."

"Why didn't he buy it?" I asked.

"Because he only buys antiques, except for a few Hopi pots and kachinas," Margaret said. "So he directed me here instead."

"Do you want the Starflowers' phone number?" I asked. "I'm sure they'd be very happy to have Sasha's ring back."

"Yes, thank you," Margaret said as I jotted down the number on some scrap paper. After sticking it in her purse, she thanked me and drifted off to inspect the rugs and baskets, while we four hurried down the hall to the café.

"So what do you think of Margaret's story?" Ned asked after we were seated. "Does it make any sense?"

"Actually it makes a lot of sense." I couldn't believe I'd just said that Margaret made sense, but in this case it was true. I paused for a moment, while we ordered lunch, then added, "At least Margaret didn't lie about Missy giving her the ring. If she'd been in on Missy's scam, Margaret might have lied to protect her. Instead, she freely admitted that Missy had given it to her to sell. I think that shows the Powells didn't team up to take the ring."

Our order of Navajo tacos arrived, and we ate for a few minutes in silence while we thought about the case. George said, "Still, the fact that Margaret told the truth about Missy having the ring doesn't prove that they didn't hurt Sasha for some other reason."

"But why would either one want to hurt her?" Bess wondered. "Margaret is way too spacey to be capable of organizing a kidnapping. And Missy is totally self-absorbed."

"They may not have deliberately hurt her," Ned said. "They may be covering up an accident, like Nancy said." I shot Ned an appreciative smile. I like it when he remembers my theories. Still, I tried to reconstruct in my imagination what might have happened at Canyonlands if the Powells weren't guilty. Sasha would have gone to investigate the noise, and someone nabbed her in the cave—maybe because she'd interrupted a theft. The Powells, who weren't exactly the sharpest pencils in the pack, didn't notice clues that would help the police. That scenario felt right to me. More and more, Andy Littlewolf made sense as my prime suspect.

After lunch, I made two phone calls, one to Mr. Starflower, who told me that he *had* mentioned our rafting trip to Mr. Littlewolf, and the other to Littlewolf's Antiques, where I got a voice mail saying that the store was open today, and Mr. Littlewolf was on the phone or with customers, but to please leave a message. Instead I hung up and asked a Gouldings desk clerk for directions to the address on his letterhead. He jotted them down and said the house was only a ten-minute drive away.

Soon the four of us had arrived at Mr. Littlewolf's hogan, which was a small circular earth and log structure typical of a Navajo dwelling. I was happy to see that there was no car in the driveway.

"I just hope his house is unlocked," I said. Not that I'm above climbing through a window to forward my investigation—I've done it on several occasions—but why go looking for trouble?

George opened the door. "Yay!" she said. "No *breaking* and entering necessary."

"Breaking and entering? I'd *never* do that," I said with a grin. "I prefer to call it *research*."

"Whatever," Bess said, as we all followed George indoors.

Mr. Littlewolf's home was very neat—*too* neat, actually. We didn't find a thing that looked suspicious or even out of place. Nothing that looked as if it belonged to Sasha. Mr. Littlewolf had a few books and Navajo baskets on a coffee table, an immaculate sofa, a kitchen with practically no food in the fridge, and a neatly made bed.

"I can't believe we drove all this way, and there's not one clue," I said. "What a disappointment." Even if Sasha wasn't here, I'd hoped to find a decent clue. I checked some drawers, but they were filled with boring stuff like tools or dishrags. "He must keep all his business papers at his store," I added. Just when I'd given up hope of finding anything, my gaze darted to a table behind the front door. It was covered with papers, and on top of the stack sat a folded sheet. I stepped over and picked it up.

It was a note. Nothing special, nothing suspicious, not even a real clue. Only a tiny lead—but better than nothing.

"Hey, guys, look at this," I said, waving the note. "It's a letter to Mr. Littlewolf at Littlewolf's Antiques confirming a room for tonight at the Hopi Cultural Center. It's probably no big deal, but . . ."

"But what?" Bess said. "Something tells me we're not done with our driving. How far away is this place?"

I grinned at Bess. She knows me too well. I couldn't let this lead hang—I just couldn't. Not with Sasha still missing. "I'm not sure how far the Cultural Center is. I know the Hopi Reservation is in northern Arizona. Why don't we call the center and get directions? The number is right on the note."

A quick phone call later, I had the directions. "It may be three hours away," I told my friends. "Are you guys on?"

"We're with you, Nancy," Ned said, and George and Bess nodded firmly. My friends are awesome.

"Don't get me wrong, guys," I said. "I'm not expecting a miracle. Mr. Littlewolf is probably just going to the Hopis to buy artifacts for his store. Then again, he may be up to something else. But it can't hurt to check out this lead. It's just a hunch."

"You've got great hunches, Nancy," Bess said cheerfully. "And if this one leads us to concrete clues about where Sasha is, I don't care how long we have to drive."

"And if it doesn't lead us to Sasha, we'll have wasted the whole day," I said.

"Nothing ventured, nothing gained," George said. "But let me ask you a practical question, Nancy. It's almost two o'clock. If the Hopi Reservation is about three hours away, don't you think we should make room reservations too? I mean, no way will we be returning to Moab tonight."

"If Andy Littlewolf is staying at the hotel tonight, then we are too," I said. "I wouldn't want to shortchange our investigation." I called the Cultural Center from the kitchen phone, charging the call to my credit card—why didn't I take my cell phone? Ergh!—and reserved two rooms for us. Minutes later we were back in the car, heading toward Arizona.

The Hopi Reservation was extremely remote, just north of Arizona's Painted Desert. The landscape didn't have the same crazy rock formations as Utah. It seemed flatter and more barren. Poorer, too. I felt bad for the people who lived there, who were obviously struggling to make a living from the dry land.

"I feel as if we've entered a different country," Ned said as our gazes fell on the countryside.

"We have," I said. "The Hopi own this land. It's their own nation, really. They've got their own laws and their own police, just like the Navajo do on their reservation. We've entered their country." Bess and George were sharing the driving on this leg of the journey, which had given me time to read up on the Hopi and Navajo in my guidebook, but I slapped it closed as we approached the Cultural Center.

Once inside, we learned that Mr. Littlewolf hadn't checked in yet.

"I have an idea," I said to my friends. "While we're waiting for him to come, let's check out the Hopi village of Walpi. The guidebook mentioned that it's the oldest occupied village in America, nearly a thousand years old. It sounds really interesting. And close, too."

"Sure," Bess said. George and Ned agreed, and soon we were driving up a treacherous winding road to the village on the mesa nearby.

"I can't look," Bess said, covering her eyes as we snaked along the narrow twisting road. But once on top, the view was stunning.

"This reminds me of a medieval town," Ned said as we parked and climbed out of the car. "It's so high up, and with its stone walls, it's almost as if it's fortified."

"My guidebook said that one reason the Hopi were able to survive here for so long is that they could spot their enemies coming," I declared. "That's exactly like a lot of medieval villages in Europe."

"Oh, look at all these dogs coming to greet us," Ned said as a pack of mangy-looking dogs ambled up to us. "Hello, guys," he added, bending down to pat a friendly black-and-brown mutt.

"They look a bit scruffy," Bess said.

A small Hopi woman in an embroidered skirt rushed up to us. "Hello there!" she said, smiling. "Please, you are all welcome here. But no patting the animals. They might carry plague."

Ned recoiled. "Excuse me? Plague?" He looked at his hand with a stricken expression.

"Yes, the dogs have fleas, and fleas sometimes carry bubonic plague in these parts," the woman told him.

"Best to go wash your hands, young man. There's a rest room in the tourist center." She led us a few doors down to a public building with a rest room. Outside the building some tables displaying kachinas and pottery were set up, but Ned didn't give them a glance as he hurried to wash his hands.

I listened to the men and women who were carving kachinas by the table chat happily away, obviously enjoying one another's company as they worked. Despite their poverty, the Hopi people seemed very close. I'd read that their spiritual beliefs are very important to them. Even though they're private about their religion, they also have a reputation for being kind and welcoming. The name Hopi, Peaceful Ones, seemed totally right to me.

"Remember what Nigel Brown, the Starflowers' friend, told us?" I whispered to Bess and George. "That the Hopi family line is tracked through the mother instead of the father."

"So I would have my mom's last name instead of my dad's?" Bess asked.

"I think so," I said.

Ned joined us, while we bought some pottery and kachina dolls. One of the kachinas was a beautiful maiden with her hair worn up in two discs around the top of her head, giving her a sort of Mickey Mouse effect. She wore soft white moccasins with leggings and a woven dress. When I lifted her up, the old man who was selling the kachinas told me she was a Snow Maiden.

On a hunch, I asked him about the Corn Ear Maidens and described the legend in Mr. Littlewolf's letter.

"Hopi mythology indeed includes that legend!" he said brightly. "Our pottery often features pictures of Corn Ear Maidens, and I even have a Corn Maiden kachina." He dug around under the table and pulled one out. The maiden wore a green mask with rainbows on the cheeks. She had bangs and long braided pigtails, and ears of corn were carved into the bottom of her shawl.

I thought about Sasha's interest in the Anasazi. If she was the recipient of Mr. Littlewolf's letter, maybe he'd written to her because of their shared interest in that culture. "Could that Hopi legend have originally been Anasazi?" I asked the man.

"I'm not sure," the man added. "Possibly."

Out of the corner of my eye, I saw Ned strolling away to explore the town. The afternoon was warm, and Ned took off his sweatshirt to wrap it around his waist. Then he leaned from the wall surrounding the town to peer down at the plain far below. Bess grabbed my arm. "I wish Ned wouldn't do that," she said. "It's making me dizzy. If he leans any farther, he'll be gone." No sooner had she finished speaking than he strolled behind the corner of a building, out of sight.

The man lifted another kachina to show me when a shout caught my attention. Ned!

Bess, George, and I froze, exchanging wide-eyed looks. He screamed again, calling my name.

I took off toward the place where I'd last seen Ned. As I charged around the corner of the building, I stopped in midrun. I couldn't believe it. On the far side of town where the road wound downhill, a red sedan roared away full throttle, with Ned's sweatshirt sleeve dragging from the back door.

The driver's tall, dark-haired shape was unmistakable. Andy Littlewolf.

12

Sinking Fast

Mr. Littlewolf was not alone. Another man sat in the rear seat. I could only see the back of his head, but I knew he wasn't Ned, since Ned was taller when he sat.

Still, Ned was in that car *somewhere*. His sweatshirt was hanging out the door.

The sedan raced down the hill, taking each hairpin turn with squeaking wheels. I sprinted toward it, struggling to make out the license plate. No luck.

"Bess! George!" I shouted, pivoting around. They were right behind me.

"Don't worry, Nancy," Bess said breathlessly. "We're with you."

I spun toward a souvenir table I'd passed on the

other side of the building. Two men were sitting behind it selling Hopi wares. "Did either of you see who was in that car?" I asked them.

They stared at me warily. Then one of the men spoke, a young heavyset guy. "I couldn't see the car—the corner blocked it from sight. But I bet that Navajo man was in it. I noticed him earlier."

"Yeah," the other man said, who was older and thinner. "He was with a white man who was acting as his intermediary."

"Intermediary?" I repeated. "You mean a go-between?" My mind clicked back to my conversation with Mr. Littlewolf when I'd suggested that he find a go-between to purchase Hopi crafts. He must have done exactly that. But who could the man be? Mr. Littlewolf had been very terse when I'd brought up the subject. He definitely hadn't mentioned any names.

"A go-between, yes," the first man said, nodding. "The Navajo man probably felt unwelcome here. See, our tribes don't exactly get along. He probably wanted to bring a neutral person to negotiate with us for our crafts. That's what I understood, anyway. I overheard a bit of their talk."

"You did?" I asked eagerly. "What else did they say?"

The older man shrugged. "Not much. I just heard

the Navajo man telling his friend that he'd feel more comfortable staying the night on his own turf, that's all. I guess he had a room at the Cultural Center and decided to cancel it."

My heart sank. Andy Littlewolf wasn't going to the Cultural Center after all. So how could I track him and Ned down? "Did either of you hear where he's planning to spend the night instead?" I asked.

"The Thunderbird Lodge in Canyon De Chelly," the younger man said. "It's in the heart of the Navajo Nation."

The older man interrupted. "The other man wanted to go to Canyon De Chelly too. He said there's something interesting in it that he wanted the Navajo man to see."

My curiosity revved up, full throttle. Something interesting in a canyon? "Did he say what it was?" I asked.

"Nope," the older man said. "The Navajo man pressed him to tell, but he gave no hint."

George cut in. "What did this guy look like?" she asked.

The men looked at each other and shrugged. The older one spoke first. "He was medium height," he said, raising his hand to his own eye level. "Middle-aged, with short brown hair and light eyes. I didn't notice their exact color. I'd never seen him before, I know that."

"Did you get his name?" Bess asked.

"No, sorry," the older man said, while the younger man shook his head.

"Did the men say anything else? Did they buy anything from you?" I asked, angling for every possible shred of information.

"They looked over our kachinas," the younger man said, "but they didn't buy any. Then they stepped away and had a big argument out of earshot. I wish I could have heard it. Then they wandered off beyond the building. A few minutes later, I heard a shout and then a car speeding away."

"Was anyone else with them?" I asked. "Like a tall guy around nineteen years old with brown hair?"

The younger man's eyes narrowed. "Navajo?"

"No," I answered. "He was with us. He was the person shouting. We think the other guys kidnapped him."

The two men looked at me in shock. "Are you sure?" the older man exclaimed. "We just assumed the shout came from one of the men arguing. I thought maybe one man had punched the other or something. But you're saying they kidnapped your friend?"

I told them about Ned's sweatshirt dragging from the back door of the car. "He yelled for me, and now he's nowhere in sight—plus, his sweatshirt is in that car," I said. "They must have kidnapped him, but we have no clue why. That's why I need to ask you these questions."

"I only wish we could be of more help," the younger man said sympathetically. "But I will call the police and report the red car for you."

"You've been a lot of help," I said, smiling my thanks. "I really appreciate everything you've done. And at least now I know where they're heading."

The men gave us directions to Canyon De Chelly. "It's over an hour east, in Arizona, close to the New Mexico border," the younger man said. "And by the way, while the name of the canyon is pronounced 'Shay,' it's spelled *C-h-e-l-l-y*. Just so you'll recognize the road signs to it."

I thanked the men, and George, Bess, and I jumped in our car. Then we sped east toward the darkening sky as the sun set behind us. "What will we do about our room at the Cultural Center?" Bess asked.

"I guess we'll just have to pay for it," I said. "I mean, we already checked in. Lucky we didn't bring any bags with us, or we'd have to come back for them. I don't want to waste a minute."

"We've got to stay on Mr. Littlewolf's trail while it's fresh," George said.

"Ned's strong," I said. "The kidnappers must have a weapon, or they never could have gotten him into their car."

"I wonder if he overheard some secret," George said, "like where Sasha is."

I wondered the same thing myself. I also wondered what was in Canyon De Chelly that was so intriguing to the mystery man. Sasha? Then I remembered the weapon. I pressed the accelerator. The sooner we arrived at Canyon De Chelly, the sooner we would discover the answers to these questions.

George broke into my thoughts. "The Hopi and Navajo don't get along, right? So maybe that's why Mr. Littlewolf used his Moab address when he made reservations at the Cultural Center—he didn't want to reveal his cultural identity."

I said, "George, you're really an excellent detective."

"I learned from the best," George said.

About an hour later we pulled into the driveway of the Thunderbird Lodge, a handsome old motel and café run by the Navajo at the mouth of Canyon De Chelly. During our trip, while there was still some light, Bess had read us the description of the canyon in the guidebook. Apparently it was a beautiful green oasis, and an important spiritual place for the Navajo. Guides regularly led tourists into it on horseback, foot, or four-wheel-drive wagons. There were several Anasazi cliff dwellings, as well as petroglyphs. But now the sky was dark, we were starving, and I was desperate to find Ned.

A quick scan of the parking lot revealed no red sedan. We climbed out of the car and anxiously filed into the reception area. But the clerk gave us disappointing news: Mr. Littlewolf had just called to cancel his reservation.

That meant they had a room for us. After calling the Navajo police, who promised to put out a search for the red sedan, we ate dinner and flopped into bed, too exhausted and upset to do anything but sleep.

The sun poured through the window, brightening my mood when I woke the next morning. Still, I knew we had our work cut out for us. I mean, two people were missing now—and one of them was Ned! Before dressing, I called the police to check in, but they'd found no sign of the red sedan, Mr. Littlewolf, Ned, Sasha, or the mystery man.

Sighing, I hung up the phone. So I would have to find them myself, with help from Bess and George.

Squaring my shoulders, I began to plan our day.

After breakfast, we booked a tour of Canyon De Chelly. The Hopi man's words stuck in my mind: There's something interesting in the canyon he wanted the Navajo man to see. I had a big hunch that a lot of our questions would be answered by whatever waited for us in that canyon.

"Hey, Nancy, did you see these pictures?" Bess asked me, nervously pointing to some photos taped to the tour desk. I took a good look.

The pictures showed various stages of a Jeep sinking in quicksand. In one shot, its roof was barely visible. In another, it had only sunk halfway. Next to the photos was a warning not to enter the canyon under any circumstances without a Navajo guide because of dangerous quicksand. Only professional guides were skilled enough to detect it.

"Was the person who drove the Jeep okay?" Bess asked the receptionist anxiously when she approached.

She nodded just as our tour was announced.

"I'm glad that driver lived," Bess murmured as she, George, and I piled into a huge open-air vehicle with a few other tourists. "Still, I don't know about venturing into this canyon. It sounds dangerous."

"It's our only lead to Ned and Sasha," I told her. "Don't worry, Bess. Our guide will protect us."

Bess looked doubtful as we bumped down the canyon's dirt roads, plowing through pools of mucky water every minute or so. Each time we crossed a stream, I could feel her tense up.

On my other side, George leaned toward me and whispered, "I kind of don't blame Bess. How can our guide tell where the quicksand is when the muddy places all look the same?"

I shrugged. "Maybe quicksand looks different from this mud, and we just haven't seen it yet."

Our thoughts were interrupted by the tour guide when he stopped the truck near some white cliff dwellings. Dressed in jeans, a cowboy hat, and boots, he told us that this was an important Anasazi ruin called the White House.

We climbed out of the truck to investigate. The dwelling had several rooms built around A.D. 1200, including an underground chamber people used for ceremonies.

"This place is so cool," George said, gazing around. "I can see why archaeologists think the Anasazi were such an advanced civilization."

As I glanced at George something red flashed through a grove of trees about a hundred yards past her. I caught my breath. Mr. Littlewolf's car? It was gone in an instant, but that didn't stop me.

"George, Bess, c'mon," I said. "I saw something

124

in the distance that could be the red sedan."

"We can sneak away now," I added, tugging on George's T-shirt sleeve. "All the other tourists are busy shopping, and the guide is helping them." As the people from our tour bargained with the Navajo women, the three of us hurried toward the grove of trees. My heart was beating a mile a minute, hoping the red flash wasn't a red herring. I didn't feel ready for a letdown.

At the edge of a small stream, Bess suddenly cried out. "Look," she gasped. "What's that?"

Pointing at a silvery gleam a few feet away, she smiled with excitement, headed toward it, then leaned down to pick it up.

I gasped as Bess held it in her palm. "It's a ranger badge, just like the one that Sasha wore!" I said.

"Awesome!" George exclaimed.

But our excitement didn't last long. Bess cried out again, this time in fear. "I'm sinking!" she yelled. "Help me, guys. Quicksand!"

She was right. It had only been seconds since she'd stepped near the stream, but the mud was inching past her knees.

13

Cave Capture

Despite her fear, Bess had amazing pluck. Summoning all her courage, she threw the badge onto firm ground.

"There!" she said. "At least the badge won't sink with me."

"You won't sink either, Bess," I said, coming as close to her as I dared. The ground under my feet was moist and suspiciously springy. Bess was about three feet away, fighting to pull herself from the quicksand.

Her eyes looked terrified. "Help me!" Bess pleaded, holding out her arms to me and George.

"Grab one arm and I'll get the other," I said to George. Together, we each held onto one of Bess's arms, then we dug in our heels and pulled.

Nothing.

"Again, Nan!" George shouted. "Before she sinks any farther." We yanked Bess until her shoulder sockets strained, but no matter how hard we pulled, the quicksand kept sucking her down, like some sort of hungry beast.

Bess screamed again. "Hurry, guys," she said. "I'm going fast. It's almost up to my hips."

George dropped Bess's arm. "I'm getting our guide," she announced. She raced off through the stand of trees, a blur of jeans and sneakers.

Something I'd read about quicksand jogged my memory. "Try not to panic, Bess. Listen to me. I've read some facts about quicksand. You've got to lie flat on your back before you sink any farther."

Bess's eyes widened. "What?"

"If you lie flat, you won't sink, and your feet will eventually rise," I said, willing myself to stay calm. I had to talk her through this and get her to relax. I just hoped my tactic would work.

Bess stared at the quicksand in horror. It was gray and slimy, and small bubbles made sucking noises as if some monstrous creature lurked underneath. A foul odor wafted up from it, making us feel sick. "I can't do this, Nancy," she moaned. "I can't lie down."

"Yes, you can, Bess. But do it now, before it's too late."

Bess shut her eyes and took a deep breath. "Okay," she breathed. "Wish me luck."

I held her hands steady as she gently lowered herself onto the surface of the quicksand. An expression of utter misery crossed her face as her back made contact with the stinky muck. Another moment and she lay perfectly horizontal across it.

She stopped sinking. Just as I predicted, her feet began to rise as her weight shifted upward. "That's right, Bess," I said soothingly. "Excellent job."

I held onto her hands the whole time, leaning across the patch of quicksand that separated us. My back was killing me as I arched over, but I had to get Bess to safety. I began to ease her along the surface toward firm ground.

Now that she lay flat, it was much easier to pull her. A big sucking noise bubbled up from the slime, like a drain unplugging, and Bess's feet were free!

"You did it, Nancy!" she cried as I skimmed her off the quicksand. The moment Bess lay safely on the ground, I dropped her hands.

"No, Bess, you did it," I said, breathing hard with relief

Bess pushed herself off the ground. "Did George find the guide?" she asked.

"I kind of hope not," I said. Now that Bess was safe, I didn't want the guide anywhere near us. I wanted to look for Ned and Sasha on our own.

Fortunately, a minute later George appeared—without the guide. "I'd almost reached him," George explained. "But then I heard that sucking sound. Then I heard a little of Bess's voice, and she sounded pretty happy. Nice work, you guys!" She stopped talking for a second to hug Bess. "Fortunately the guide didn't hear you guys—I guess he was too busy. Everyone was getting back into the vehicle, but no one saw me, and the guide isn't taking attendance."

"Excellent." I mopped Bess's back with the sweatshirt I kept in my backpack, then added, "Now, where were we?"

The badge.

I picked it up, and it flashed in the sunlight. I had this odd hunch it was trying to tell me something.

I turned it around, and my heart leaped. A small piece of paper was stuck onto the pin in back. George and Bess looked on as I slid the paper off.

I held it up for all to see. A name had been written there in shaky pink lipstick: Nigel.

A lightbulb went off in my brain. I turned to my friends.

"Remember that dinner we had in Moab with Nigel Brown, the old friend of Sasha's mother?" I asked them.

"Sure. He's that British archaeologist, the expert in Indian artifacts," George replied.

"Well, this must be the same Nigel," I said. "I mean, Nigel isn't exactly a common name around here." I took another look at the note. The *l* looked shaky, as if the writer had been interrupted while finishing.

"Sasha must have dropped her badge here on purpose as a clue," Bess said. "She's probably nearby."

Our gazes scanned the area. I knew that Canyon De Chelly stretched deep into the land, and at one point it forked. If Ned and Sasha were really here, they could be hidden in any one of a zillion nooks in this endless place. And it was so remote that no one would ever hear them cry for help. At least it was cooler and greener than Canyonlands. I felt hopeful. Maybe they could survive if someone was bringing them food and water.

"Nigel!" George exclaimed, her voice full of wonder. "Who would have thought? But why would he kidnap Sasha and Ned?"

"I think he kidnapped Sasha because she interrupted him doing something illegal," I said.

"In Canyonlands?" Bess asked.

I nodded. "Maybe he was stealing Anasazi artifacts from that cave—the one where I found Mr. Littlewolf's note."

"Wait a sec, I don't get it," Bess said, frowning. "Why would a letter with Mr. Littlewolf's name have been in that cave? What does he have to do with all this?"

I fished the letter from my pocket and studied it. "I bet Mr. Littlewolf wrote this letter to Nigel. Maybe Mr. Littlewolf was never even in the cave. Nigel probably had it with him and dropped it by mistake while he was raiding the place."

"But Mr. Littlewolf must be involved somehow," George said. "I mean, we saw him driving the red car. With Ned inside!"

"Oh yeah," Bess said. "He's involved up to his eyeballs."

Once more I scanned Mr. Littlewolf's letter, then looked back at my friends. "If Mr. Littlewolf wrote this letter to Nigel—and let's assume for now that he did—why would he have written him about the Corn Maiden legend?" I asked.

George shrugged. "Maybe Nigel and Littlewolf are a team, and they needed to know about the legend."

"A team of what, though?" I asked. "Thieves, kidnappers? What are they after?"

"Maybe they're after something to do with the Hopi tribe," Bess said.

I was intrigued. Though it sometimes seems as if

Bess only cares about clothes, desserts, and flirting, she can take you by surprise with her sharp observations—stuff that other people don't always see. "But Bess, why the Hopi?" I asked. "Why not the Navajo? After all, Mr. Littlewolf is Navajo, and Sasha and Nigel are here in Canyon De Chelly. Or at least, they were."

Bess hesitated, gathering her thoughts, then said, "Remember, Mr. Littlewolf didn't feel welcome on Hopi land without a neutral person. As a Navajo, Littlewolf needed Mr. Brown to cool things for him at the Hopi Reservation. So maybe they teamed up to do something there."

"I see why Andy needed Nigel. But why would Nigel need Andy?" George asked. "How would the team benefit him?"

"And how does Ned figure in?" I asked.

Bess shrugged. "He might have overheard something they wanted to keep secret."

The three of us were silent for a moment, mulling over all these possibilities. But we couldn't waste another moment theorizing. Ned and Sasha were missing, and we had to find them.

My gaze shifted to some cliffs on our right. The rock face was broken by thin crevices slicing downward. If you weren't looking carefully, you might assume they were just shadows. Nodding toward the cliffs, I said, "See those openings? If I were Nigel or Andy, I'd consider those prime hiding places."

"Let's hike closer," George suggested. "That's not such a far-fetched thought. Sasha's badge was found just a couple hundred yards away."

"And don't forget the red sedan," I added. "My gut tells me that red flash was it." We marched toward the cliffs, and I inspected some dried mud along the way. "Look guys. Tire tracks and footprints in the mud. Big ones and small."

"Sasha's?" George asked.

"Maybe," I replied.

Soon we reached the nearest cliff, the one with the most crevices. As I stared up at it my heart sank. There were so many crevices. I didn't have a clue which one to search first.

Not knowing what else to do, I yelled Ned's name, then Sasha's. George and Bess joined in. Our voices echoed eerily off the canyon walls.

And then, amazingly, we heard a response. I knew it wasn't an echo. Ned and Sasha were shouting back from a crevice on our right!

Bess, George, and I grabbed each other in excitement. "There!" I exclaimed, pointing. We made a beeline for the crevice, climbing up to it boulder by boulder like mountain goats. Just outside, we paused for breath—and then I saw the red sedan! Parked far below us, half hidden in a patch of brush, it seemed vaguely sinister, like a wild animal sleeping. Not a hint of movement disturbed the bushes around it.

"Watch out, guys!" George said, pointing to the left. A large boulder leaned precariously by the crevice, looking as if the slightest breeze could cause it to topple and seal the opening.

"Come on," I whispered.

Gingerly we slipped inside. The cave was black. I couldn't see my hand in front of me. But that didn't matter, because I could hear.

"Nancy!" Ned exclaimed, his familiar voice ringing through the darkness. "I can't believe you found us."

"Bess and George, too," Sasha said joyfully. "You're amazing!"

In a moment my eyes adjusted. Ned and Sasha were sitting on the cave floor, their legs shackled to an iron bar in the wall. I rushed over to give them hugs, followed by Bess and George.

But wait. Did I see *three* prisoners? I blinked, and the image sharpened. Farther back in the cave, Andy Littlewolf sat in the dim light, his legs shackled to the same iron bar.

But before I could speak to him, his eyes shifted from me to the space behind me. My skin prickled.

A noise crunched near the cave opening. Footsteps! I pivoted toward them. Against the bright blue of the entrance, a dark silhouette loomed up.

"So, girls, we meet again," a British voice snickered.

14

The Stolen Relic

Silence filled the cave. You could have heard a pin drop. In the dim light, I could barely make out Bess and George's tense faces, but I knew what they were thinking: *How do we get out of this one?*

A kerosene lamp flared up. In the sudden brightness I watched Nigel set it down on the cave floor next to his backpack.

Andy Littlewolf eyed him with loathing. "Thief!" he cried. "You tricked me!"

"Littlewolf, put a lid on it," Nigel said in a bored tone. "I've heard enough complaints from you to last me a lifetime. Thank goodness I'm flying back to England today."

"You'd better let us go first," Mr. Littlewolf said. "You promised you would."

"Promises are made to be broken," Nigel proclaimed. "But before I seal you people up in this cave to rot forever, let me show you why it's all been worth it." He reached inside his backpack and pulled out a wad of newspaper. Then he lovingly peeled it back to reveal a beautiful earthenware pot about eight inches wide. "Can everyone see the picture on it?" Nigel asked.

I crept closer, curious, following George, who also wanted a peek. On one side of the pot under a geometric pattern was an illustration of a Corn Ear Maiden, similar to the kachina we'd seen at the Hopi Reservation.

"Be careful," Sasha said. "He has a knife."

Nigel turned the pot as we backed away slightly. On the other side was a coyote. "This is an exceedingly rare pot," Nigel said. "Not only is it unbroken, but it shows a link between the Hopi and Anasazi cultures through the Corn Maiden myth. It will make my gallery in London famous! My gallery will be a major showcase for pre-Columbian American art outside of the United States."

"But you stole that pot," Andy said bitterly. "And you forced me to make your theft legal."

Nigel smirked. "What good would the pot do just sitting in a cave for the rest of eternity? Much better to bring the achievements of the Anasazi to the world's attention."

"It wasn't yours to take," Mr. Littlewolf said. "You found it on federal land. It's a Native American possession, not yours."

"But the only people who know I stole it will be sealed up in here," he declared. "The moment I leave, I'll give that boulder outside a push. Gravity will do the rest of the work for me." He chuckled. "Hey, the world won't know I'm a thief. They'll just think I'm a clever collector."

"You'll be a murderer," Sasha said, "if you trap us in this cave."

"Whether I'm a thief or a murderer makes no difference to me," Nigel said. "What's important is that the world will never know."

"How can you do this?" Sasha moaned. "You're one of my mother's oldest friends."

"Don't make me feel guilty," Nigel said. "Your mother is a delight, Sasha, but I don't want to do jail time. This little theft of mine got a bit out of hand, and now too many people know about it. It's your fault really, my dear, for catching me red-handed in Canyonlands."

I couldn't listen anymore. It was too frustrating to hear Nigel trying to justify his crimes. And even though I was curious to learn the details of the case, like how Andy and Nigel are connected and why Ned had been kidnapped, I knew we were running out of time. Nigel was putting his pot away, still blocking the cave entrance. At any moment, though, he could leave, and we'd be sealed inside.

I did a quick scan of the cave. Was there anything here I could use as a weapon? There were no sticks that I could see, just a stone the size of my hand on the ground between Nigel and George. But even if I'd had a weapon, Nigel stood between us and the entrance. The second he sensed trouble, he'd just run outside and seal the cave.

I thought fast. There was no way I could fight him, but maybe I could outsmart him. There was one thing I didn't fully understand—why Mr. Littlewolf had written to Nigel about the Corn Maiden legend. But I knew it had to be important to Nigel, or he wouldn't have taken the letter with him into Canyonlands, and he wouldn't be so captivated by the particular pot that he'd stolen. My mind clicked back to the basic facts of the legend. The nice Blue Corn Maiden became a coyote, and the treacherous Yellow Corn Maiden became a snake.

In as calm a voice as I could manage, I began to speak to Nigel. "I read about the Corn Ear Maidens, Mr. Brown. It's an interesting story."

Nigel perked up. "Ah, Nancy, which story do you mean? There are several legends about Corn Maidens, you know."

"I think it's called 'The Revenge of the Blue Corn Ear Maiden.' The Blue Maiden turns into a coyote, and the Yellow Maiden becomes a snake after they trick each other."

"Ah, trickery! A most admirable quality," Nigel said, casting a gloating look toward Mr. Littlewolf.

I spoke fast, before Nigel could get distracted. "Mr. Brown, I'm guessing your pot shows the Blue Corn Ear Maiden because she turned into a coyote. So wouldn't a pot with a drawing of the Yellow Corn Ear Maiden and a snake be a perfect match for yours?"

Nigel's eyes gleamed with interest. "It certainly would. But I doubt such a rarity exists."

"Oh, but it does," I told him, fudging. I couldn't believe such an intelligent man was buying this. He was probably exhausted by all of his lying and cheating. "Just before you came, I found a pot in this cave with that very picture on it. It's about the same size as your pot."

"Impossible!" Nigel snorted.

"No, it's true. I mean, the Anasazi lived here in Canyon De Chelly. So why wouldn't they have made a pot like that? I mean, they made yours, didn't they? Here, take a look. I've got it in my backpack."

Greed flickered in his eyes, and I could tell I'd actually caught him. I held my breath as he came closer, deeper into the cave, past George and Bess. I stalled for time, rummaging through my backpack, pretending I was looking for the pot. He knelt down next to me, totally absorbed.

I sneaked a look back at George, then nodded toward the stone on the cave floor. Her face brightened with understanding.

"Here, Mr. Brown, you can judge whether these two pots make a pair," I said, still fishing in my pack.

"I can't believe you found such a pot. What an extraordinary find," he said. He peered into my backpack, completely unsuspecting of what lurked behind him.

With the stone in her hand, George paused behind Nigel for a split second, judging her aim. I held my breath, hoping he wouldn't turn around, praying he wouldn't realize my ruse. Because if he did, we'd be sunk. Or more accurately, we'd be buried alive.

But before another moment passed, George raised the stone. Out of the corner of my eye, I watched as George rescued us from a very grim fate. In one fluid motion, she brought the stone down on Nigel's head, and he slumped to the cave floor, unconscious.

"I didn't hit him very hard," George said anxiously. "I didn't want to seriously hurt him. He's going to come around any second."

Sure enough, he'd already begun to moan and stir. "Nancy, get his keys," Ned said. "They're in his pocket. Unlock our cuffs, and lock him up instead. Quick!"

I acted fast, and when Nigel came to a few moments later, he found his ankle chained to the same bar that had once held his prisoners. Surprise filled his face as they now stood over him, free.

"So the tables are turned, Nancy Drew," Nigel murmured as he struggled to stand. He immediately sat back against the wall, his face pale with the effort. He touched the back of his head and winced. "You tricked me, Nancy. I give you credit for that. It's not easy to pull the wool over the eyes of Nigel Brown."

"I guess you're usually the one to fool people, Mr. Brown, judging from what Andy Littlewolf had said," I threw back. "Now maybe you'll tell us what your relationship with Mr. Littlewolf is. Were you guys a team? And did you double-cross him?"

"We were never a team, Nancy!" Mr. Littlewolf blurted out in a shocked tone. "I'm no thief. But he *did* force me to sign some papers."

I frowned. "What papers?"

"Let me clarify that," Nigel said. "Nancy, I see you don't know everything, so I'll fill you in. As you are aware, I've been looking for clues linking the Hopi and Anasazi cultures, and I've become fascinated with Hopi legends and whether they trickled down from the Anasazi. So when I found that pot in the

Canyonlands cave, I figured it must be about the same Hopi legend. I wanted the pot for my gallery, but I needed papers showing that I owned it in case anyone ever asked. And that's where Andy Littlewolf came in." He shot Mr. Littlewolf a taunting look.

"So you *were* a team," George said.

"Never!" Mr. Littlewolf said angrily.

"We were a team of sorts," Nigel went on. "We knew each other in Moab because we were both interested in Indian antiquities and legends. When I first stumbled across my pot, I didn't have a way to conceal it and remove it safely from the cave. Upon returning to Moab, I asked Andy if he knew of a legend involving a corn maiden and a coyote. He did a bit of research, then wrote me a note describing the legend, which he knew to be Hopi. So I returned to the cave, realizing this pot was a rare find indeed. I took the pot, but inadvertently dropped the note. Fortunately I'd torn my name off in case I happened to lose it, so no one could link me with the theft. See, it was quite possible someone else knew the pot was there."

"But you still haven't told us why Mr. Littlewolf was your prisoner," Bess said.

"Patience, patience," Nigel replied. "All in good time. When Andy wanted to visit the Hopi Reservation to buy stuff for his store, he asked me to come with him as a go-between to negotiate for him on unfriendly territory. Naturally, after I did him that favor, I figured he owed me one."

I put two and two together. "So you then asked him to say in a letter that the pot had been his and he'd sold it to you legitimately."

Nigel nodded at me respectfully. "You're beginning to understand, Nancy. Yes, I asked him to write me such a letter." He shot a wicked look at Mr. Littlewolf. "Yet he had the nerve to refuse me!"

"So you argued in the Hopi village," I guessed. "And Ned overheard, so you kidnapped him."

"Andy was being stubborn," Nigel declared. "Since he wouldn't write me a letter, I decided to lure him here and force him to write it by threatening to hurt Sasha. But Ned presented an opportunity earlier."

"You mean you kidnapped Ned just to force Mr. Littlewolf to write the letter for you?" I asked.

"Well, he was snooping," Nigel said, as if it was all Ned's fault. "I had to silence him for that alone. But I also used Ned to force Andy's hand."

"Nigel ordered me into the car at knifepoint," Ned explained. "He made Mr. Littlewolf drive, and threatened to hurt me if he wouldn't obey. Nigel forced us to come here, where he'd already brought Sasha."

"That's right," Mr. Littlewolf said. "With both

Sasha and Ned under threat, I finally wrote the letter Nigel needed. But by then it was too late. We all knew too much about him, so he wouldn't let us go."

"So once he got the letter, he didn't need you anymore. He decided he'd be better off without you," Bess said. "How coldhearted is that?"

I felt sickened by Nigel. He was willing to sacrifice lives for his own glory. And Sasha was the daughter of his old friend! I couldn't let him see how angry I was, though. Not yet. Not if I wanted him to answer all my questions about the case.

"Tell me about the raft," I said. "You put the knife in it, right?"

"I certainly did," he said proudly. "I happened to be at Littlewolf's Antiques talking to Andy when Paul Starflower called and mentioned, among other things, that you were going rafting. I listened in on the phone extension. See, I knew you were on the case, Nancy, because Paul and Kate mentioned it before we all met for dinner that evening in Moab."

"So you slipped away from the store to plant the knife?" George asked.

"It was an opportunity, shall we say," Nigel said smugly. "I would have been foolish not to try. River Outfitters was just down the street, and the raft had already been strapped to the trailer outside. You were inside taking care of last minute business with the

145

guide, so I just . . . acted. Luckily I had some yellow tape on me; I'd been patching up my own raft earlier that day. I wanted to get you out of my way, Nancy. I knew you'd find Sasha sooner or later. And I knew you'd find me."

"Well, you were right about that," Ned said. "But why did you take us to this cave? Why not one in Canyonlands where Sasha had surprised you?"

"I knew people would be searching Canyonlands for her, so I drove her here instead," he replied. "I tossed her into my Jeep, which I'd hidden at the top of the cliff, and sped to Canyon De Chelly more than three hours away. I'd discovered this cave a few weeks ago while searching for artifacts. It was a perfect hiding place for a hostage. The iron bar had probably been used for tethering animals at one time, but I saw no sign that the cave had been occupied in years."

"But Sasha is the daughter of your friends," I said. "Don't you feel any loyalty?"

"Of course I do, Nancy," Nigel said. "Do you think I'm *that* hard-hearted? I planned to tell Paul and Kate where she was, once I was safely out of the country. I thought prosecution unlikely, especially because there were no witnesses. And I was willing to sacrifice our friendship to get the pot. But when Ned and Andy became involved, the game changed. I couldn't let them go without risking my freedom.

There were simply too many witnesses."

"So why are you here now?" I asked him. "You've already got your letter."

"To check the cave for artifacts one last time. But you foiled me, Nancy. I should be at the airport by now." He glared at me with his cold gray eyes, and despite the heat, a chill ran through me. But at least he was right about one thing: We were all okay.

After the police arrested Nigel, we happily returned to Moab. The Starflowers were thrilled to be reunited with Sasha, but they were also horrified by Nigel's crimes. Mrs. Starflower couldn't believe that Nigel had done such terrible things, and that she'd been in the dark for so long about his real personality.

"I'd always known he was ambitious," she said, "but I never dreamed he'd go to such extremes. And use such treachery!"

The Powells barely noticed Sasha's return, except when Missy reluctantly gave back her ring, but Nick was ecstatic to see her again. The funny thing was that Sasha seemed happy to see him, too. And our first evening back, as she and Nick sat at a table for two at the Laughing Tortilla, I got the feeling that they really cared about each other. All Nick needed was a little more confidence that Sasha liked him, and a better grip on his temper.

Bess, George, Ned, and I sat with Mr. and Mrs. Starflower at another table. The Starflowers were so nice, thanking me for my detective work. But I don't think of solving mysteries as work. For me, they're exciting adventures, like the mountain biking trip my friends and I were planning the next day on some nearby trails.

"If anyone hears a strange noise when we're out on the trails tomorrow, don't investigate!" Ned warned.

"Why not?" George said. "Nancy can deal with it."

"Hey, wait a minute! I'd kind of like to relax too," I said, smiling.

"You *always* say that," Bess said, raising her soda glass in a toast, "but we know better."

REDISCOVER THE CLASSIC MYSTERIES OF NANCY DREW

star power

by Catherine Hapka

She's beautiful, she's talented, she's famous.

She's a star!

Things would be perfect
if only her family
was around to help
her celebrate. . . .

Follow the
adventures of
fourteen-year-old
pop star
Star Calloway

Have you read all of the Alice Books?